In an Instant

Tracy Wainwright

In an Instant
COPYRIGHT 2019 by Tracy Wainwright

Contact Information: titleadmin@pelicanbookgroup.com

All scripture quotations, unless otherwise indicated, are taken from the Holy Bible, New International Version(R), NIV(R), Copyright 1973, 1978, 1984, 2011 by Biblica, Inc.™ Used by permission of Zondervan. All rights reserved worldwide. www.zondervan.com

Cover Design: Nicola Martinez

Prism is a division of Pelican Ventures, LLC
www.pelicanbookgroup.com PO Box 1738 *Aztec, NM * 87410

The Triangle Prism logo is a trademark of Pelican Ventures, LLC

Publishing History
Prism Edition, 2019
Paperback Edition ISBN 978-1-5223-9859-2
Electronic Edition ISBN 978-1-5223-9858-5
Published in the United States of America

Dedication

To Gary: Thank you for loving me no matter what.

ONE

A demanding voice broke through Terrence's concentration.

"I don't care if your policy says to wait forty-eight hours. I want someone to help me look for my wife."

He glanced up from the stack of paperwork to the man berating the front desk clerk. Late twenties, he guessed. About five foot ten, dark blond hair, fit. Probably worked with his hands, judging from the calluses visible on his palms from across the room. The man's face shone beet red, and he glared at the poor rookie. Jack turned from the angry man and met Terrence's gaze. He raised his eyebrows and widened his eyes.

Terrence groaned, handed the file he'd been flipping through to Officer Clark, and sauntered over.

The distraught man shifted his gaze to meet his straight on. Terrence ignored the pain reflected in the man's eyes. Anyone could fake emotion.

"What's the problem, sir?" He steadied his voice, exuding calm instead of the irritation bubbling inside.

The best way to get someone to placidity was to lead them there.

The man spoke through clenched teeth. "My...wife...is...missing. I want someone to help me find her."

"OK. Let's start with the basics. What's your name?"

"Luke Montgomery. My wife's name is Julie."

He held the man's challenging stare. Mr. Montgomery refocused the conversation off himself and back to his wife. Interesting. Most missing wife cases turned out to be the husband. Deflection could be a cover. "OK. Your wife is missing. How long has she been gone?"

"About two hours."

He blinked several times instead of rolling his eyes as he wanted. Montgomery's wife probably decided to take a long breakfast with a girlfriend or do some early morning Christmas shopping. The possibilities were endless. "Two hours? She could be anywhere, passing time, goofing off with a friend." He took a deep breath. "Give her some more time. She'll show up, and you'll laugh about it over turkey in a couple weeks."

Terrence turned to leave, but a hand gripped the sleeve of his uniform, spinning him back around. Heat seared through his veins. "Remove your hand, sir."

Tears pooled in the man's eyes, throwing Terrence off balance. He stepped back, and Mr. Montgomery let go of his shirt.

"You don't get it." Mr. Montgomery raked his fingers through his hair. "She should be at work. Her car's where she always parks it. She's as reliable as a clock. She's missing, and I know every minute ticking by means the chances of finding her diminishes."

Terrence's blood cooled to a simmer. He glanced at Jack and met sympathy in the young cop's eyes. Great. This guy isn't going away until someone talks to him. "All right, Mr. Montgomery. Why don't we get some coffee, sit down, and tell me about your wife."

The man's shoulders dropped. "Thank you."

He turned to the rookie. "Jack?"

"Interview room two is open."

"This way, Mr. Montgomery." Terrence led him through the desks, paused to fill two cups of coffee, then continued down a hallway and into the room with a large "2" pasted on the door. He closed the door, flicked his hand toward the metal chair on the opposite side of the table, and plunked down. He glanced behind him. Jack would have sent someone to observe from the other side of the two-way mirror in case this guy got a little too passionate about his missing wife.

He sipped from one of the steaming cups and set the extra one on the table in front of the troubled Mr. Montgomery. The man shook his head.

"OK, tell me more about your wife. When did you last see or talk to her?"

Montgomery splayed his fingers flat on the cold, hard table and stared at them. "About six-thirty when she left for work."

"What about before that? Did y'all have a fight?" He slurped from his cup again. Black and strong. How he perceived himself. How he preferred his coffee.

Montgomery's jaw twitched. "No. The morning went great. Nothing seemed out of the ordinary until her coworker Sue called to say Julie never showed up."

He studied the man. Creased brow, open arms. He didn't appear to be hiding anything.

Terrence leaned back in his chair and ran his thumb along the top rim of the Styrofoam. "Let's go back to before she left. Give me the play-by-play of the morning."

The muscles in Montgomery's face relaxed, and he also leaned back. "We got up at five and went for a run, like we do every weekday morning. I fixed breakfast while she took a shower. We ate together, and she finished getting ready while I showered. We kissed good-bye, got in our cars, and headed to work."

Ugh. How disgustingly bland. No one could be that boring. He had to be leaving something out. "But she never made it."

He scrunched his eyebrows. "No."

"And her coworker called to tell you?" Terrence drained the rest of the bitter coffee.

"Yes, our friend Sue works with her. When she hadn't shown up by seven thirty, a half hour late, she texted me."

"Um hmm."

"I texted and called Julie, but she never answered. I left my job site and went to hers. I found her car in the parking lot in her usual location. I followed the path she walks every day to her shop. Sue was there, busy getting ready for the day. She hadn't seen or heard a word from Julie. Nothing." Tears filled his eyes, and he released a shuddering sigh. "It's like one instant she was there and the next she was gone."

Terrence tapped his fingertips together. The man certainly gave a good impression of being worried. If someone had abducted this woman and she hadn't simply decided to take a break, she made it simple. A creature of habit. They were the easiest to scout. A stalker had no problem tracking down and finding an effortless path to a person who never varied from routine. Terrence didn't believe in deviating from the law, but in matters of patterns and habits, doing things differently not only kept things interesting, but could also keep someone safe.

He needed time to think.

"You gonna drink that coffee?"

The grieved man shook his head.

Terrence reached for the cup. A tepid sip bought him a few more seconds. Under most circumstances, he wouldn't even consider following up on something like this. They didn't start investigating a missing person unless much more time had passed. Or they found evidence of foul play. A wife didn't show up for work, but her car did. She followed the same routine every day, until today. It could be a case of a bored woman in need of escape. Except for the car.

An affair was always a possibility. A secret plan to sneak off with a boyfriend. It'd been known to happen.

"You contacted anyone else? See if she's talked to someone?"

"Sue texted a couple of friends but tried not to scare them. I called Julie's mom. Asked her what time we're supposed to take her to dinner later this week for her birthday, so I could schedule a job. She said nothing about Julie, so I knew she hadn't talked to her. There's no one else to call. Not without alerting everyone she's missing." Mr. Montgomery lowered his head bracing it with his hands.

Not bad. He didn't seem to be some ignorant, overly trusting husband. But still, a missing person in two hours was a hard sell. "No other family? No one else Julie might contact if something upset her?"

"No. Her dad's been out of the picture for twenty years, and she doesn't have any siblings. Something's happened." His voice cracked, and he glanced up. "Please. Help me find my wife."

Logic told Terrence to stick to protocol. Nothing specifically screamed foul play. But he hadn't looked for any evidence either. Maybe he could go to the work site and check things out. The trip wouldn't take up too much time and nothing else pressed him at the moment. Just paperwork waited for him that morning.

"You said job site. Where do you work?"

"I'm a carpenter. I'm working at a house in Queen's Lake right now."

"And your wife?"

"Julie works at Colonial Williamsburg. She's an interpreter at one of the small houses." He leaned forward. "She loves her job. She wouldn't miss a day on her own accord. She's never even taken a sick day."

"All right. You've caught me on a slow day. As long as nothing else comes over the line, I can ride out with you and take a look around."

Mr. Montgomery's eyes widened, and his eyebrows lifted. "You believe me? You're going to look for her?"

"I can't promise anything, but I'll check it out." Terrence stood.

The man reached across the table, grasped his hand, and shook it. "Thank you. Thank you so much."

~*~

Terrence steered his cruiser into the busy parking lot and pulled in three spots down from Mr. Montgomery. Plucking his pad and pen out of his pocket, he stepped out of the car and locked the door. "Where's your wife's car?"

"Not here. Julie parks in an employee parking lot."

OK. I get it. Mr. Montgomery wanted him to use her name. Making it more personal. "Can you show me where it is?" He followed in silence as they wove through the old buildings and across several streets, some open to traffic, some not, to a gravel lot labeled Employee Parking Only.

Mr. Montgomery stopped by a red Honda Civic about ten years old. "This is it."

Terrence noted the car's condition, location, and license plate in his book. He inspected the ground around the car. No rocks scraped or piled. No signs of a struggle. He peeked in the windows. A Bible sat on the passenger seat. Other than that, the car held no clutter. Not one receipt, discarded fast food bag, or sales ad. "Her car always this clean?"

A grin broke through the man's concern. "Yes. Julie's methodical. I told you. Same schedule. Same parking spot. Same thing every day. She's predictable."

"Hmm." That may be what got her in trouble, if she was in trouble. "Do you have a key?"

Mr. Montgomery dug in his pocket, flipped through a set of keys, and handed Terrence the one with a black gripper on the end.

Unlocking the door, he slid into the driver's seat with his legs turned out. Mrs. Montgomery wasn't very tall. He'd have had to move the seat several inches back to accommodate his long legs. He reached under the seat. Nothing. He dug into the storage compartment that doubled as a console. A handful of CDs, a map, and some index cards. He flipped through the index cards. Half were blank. The others had Bible verses written on them. He replaced them and closed the hatch. Next, he inspected the glove box. The manual from the manufacturer, some napkins, and a couple of cards completed his inventory. A quick perusal of the cards showed they were keepsakes from Mr. Montgomery.

He rolled his eyes. No one could be this neat and squeaky clean. He patted the floor under the passenger seat and pulled out an umbrella. An inspection of the backseat proved fruitless. Not one thing out of place.

He pulled the lever to pop the trunk and walked around to the back of the car and peered in. Two wrapped packages were held in by a flexible netting in the trunk. He checked the tags. *To my one and only love, L. Your wife, J.*

His face was hidden from Mr. Montgomery, so he didn't hold back the grimace. Overly ritualized and sappy sweet. He closed the trunk and handed the keys back to their owner. "Everything looks fine here. Can you show me the building where she works?"

"Sure." He locked the car and turned to cross the parking lot.

Terrence kept his attention alert to the route. He didn't come to Colonial Williamsburg often. Hadn't been there since his last field trip in middle school. He'd never been a fan of history. It didn't take going back too far into the past until things got ugly and he got mad. No, CW would never make it on his list of favorite places to go. Although, he had to admit the holiday decorations adorning all the buildings and street lamps reminded him of the fresh cookies his mom baked every year in preparation for Christmas. He made a mental note to call her once he'd convinced Montgomery he had nothing to worry about.

"This is it," the man told him.

Terrence scanned the small building. Like many of the others, wreaths and garland called travelers in. The smell of cinnamon wafting from inside made the invitation nearly impossible to resist. His growling stomach reminded him he'd skipped breakfast. Too bad Julie Montgomery didn't work in one of the taverns, so he could order something to eat.

He ducked his head and stepped inside. A pale, soft skinned woman dressed in eighteenth century garb grinned a greeting from behind a weaver's wheel. Her gaze shifted to Luke, and her smile faded. Tears welled in her eyes. She blinked them away and pasted the smile back on as she wrapped up a discussion on traditional weave with the couple of older ladies watching her work.

"Thank you." A woman in a gray jacket glanced over her shoulder at the two men, her eyes grazing over Terrence's uniform. She tugged on her friend's arm and quickly exited through a second door.

Terrence met the young woman's gaze. "You're Sue?"

"Yes." She let the wheel go still, yarn resting on her legs. "You're here about Julie? I'm really worried."

"I understand she's usually here by seven?"

"Yes. Every day. I always run late." She blushed and looked at her hands, resting on her swollen stomach. "But not Julie. She's always here on time and gets things started." Her tear-filled eyes met his. "Something's wrong. I know it."

"When did you talk to her last?"

"Last night around eight. We were planning her mom's birthday dinner for later this week. Ms. Fran has adopted us all, and we were going to take her out to celebrate."

He raised his eyebrows. "Us all?"

"Yeah. Several of us who've been friends for several years."

"Her mom's last name?"

She glanced at Luke then answered. "Byers."

He scribbled the name in his notebook. "And Julie

seemed OK. Nothing was wrong? She didn't appear concerned or upset about anything?"

Sue scrunched up her nose. "No. She sounded tired, but we'd had a long day. Julie was excited. She'd ordered balloons and flowers and made the reservations for dinner on Thursday. I tried texting her this morning at least a dozen times. She never answered. That's not like her." A lone tear escaped and trickled down her cheek.

"Did you talk to any of the other workers? Ask if anyone saw her?"

"A few. We don't have a chance to socialize outside of breaks and lunch. We all keep to our own buildings once the work day starts."

He clicked his pen shut. A dead end. No one had seen this woman. Nothing at her car indicated foul play. She simply hadn't shown up for work. She deviated from the norm for a break, and the people around her weren't used to that. He closed his notebook. "Thanks, ma'am. I appreciate it." He turned to Luke. "I think that's about it."

"That's it? You're not –"

"You here about Julie?"

Terrence swiveled toward the voice coming from the open doorway. The young man staring back at him couldn't have been a day over nineteen. He wore a fife costume, complete with white breeches, red coat, and black tri-corner hat. Must be a musician. "You are?"

"Ken."

"Do you know anything about Mrs. Montgomery's whereabouts?"

"I'm not sure. The rumor mill just got around to me, and I came by to see if she'd shown up. We all love Mrs. Julie."

Biting his tongue, Terrence held back a chastisement. Youth. They always wanted to be involved in something exciting. "So you don't have any pertinent information?"

The boy shrugged, his hands quivering. "I don't know…"

Terrence tapped his foot. "OK. What do you know?"

"I didn't think anything about it, but on my way to work this morning, I found a Starbucks coffee cup on the path. I picked it up and threw it away."

Sue gasped, covering her mouth with her hands.

Luke paled.

Terrence studied their faces. "A coffee cup. Does that mean something?"

"Julie–" Luke cleared his throat. "Julie always stopped at Starbucks on her way to work. Always."

Terrence flipped open the notebook and clicked out his pen. "Where was this cup?"

"A few doors down, that way." He motioned the direction Terrence and Luke had come from.

"Show me."

Four buildings down Ken stopped in the path. The pool of coffee had been trampled, but the cold had kept it in place. He noted the location in his book. "And where did you throw the cup away?"

"Over there." Ken pointed to a trash can across the path.

He walked over and peeked in. Trash. He really should carry gloves at all times. He had plenty stashed back in his car. He pulled a flashlight from his belt and peered in. Sure enough, half of a white paper cup with a green logo peeked through a handful of discarded items. Now he was glad he hadn't waited until later in the day to pursue this. The hour still being early just became a benefit. "Ken. Go find me a clean plastic bag."

Moments later the enthusiastic youth returned. Using the plastic bag, Terrence reached in and retrieved the cup. A lipstick stain shone on the rim, ensuring he'd get DNA. Hopefully, prints, too. He turned to the young man. "I'm going to need you to come back to my car to give me fingerprint samples. I'll need to compare them with anything we find to isolate them from Mrs. Montgomery's or any others."

Ken stared.

"You need to tell anyone?"

"Oh. Yeah. I'll be right back." He sped off.

"You won't find Julie's prints," Luke voiced, heavy with emotion.

"No?"

"She'd have had gloves on."

Of course. "We'll still check. Do you have a hairbrush with some hair in case we don't get prints? We can most likely get DNA from her lipstick imprint."

A weak smile crept on Luke's face. "No. The hair will be in the trash. She cleans her brush every morning, but it'll be there." The smile faded. He reached out but stopped short of grasping Terrence's arm and let his fall to his side. Hope and desperation mixed in the lines creasing his brow. "You think something happened to her? You believe me."

He inspected the plastic encased cup in his hand. "A dropped coffee cup doesn't mean much."

Luke Montgomery's eyes beseeched him.

Normally, none of this would warrant investigation. If only Julie Montgomery hadn't been such a creature of habit. He sighed. "I'll look into it."

TWO

Luke eased up behind the three tourists interested in Sue's weaving demonstration. She prattled on, although less enthusiastically than she normally would, describing her technique and the history behind it. His gaze shifted to the second wheel, which sat still and cold. His chest tightened and his nose burned as he fought a new set of tears. Where could Julie be? No one had any reason to kidnap her. He shook his head and swallowed the growing lump in his throat. It didn't make sense. But neither did her not showing up for work.

As a carpenter, life seldom stayed predictable. He'd always liked it that way. New jobs. Carving wood to create houses, kitchens, furniture. Something different to do every week if not every day.

He swallowed again and stepped forward, catching Sue's gaze as she answered questions.

He glanced away. He couldn't stand to think about never seeing Julie again. Too many hours spent watching crime shows haunted him. Women brutally abused and murdered for some sicko's pleasure.

He flung away the images. He couldn't allow himself to go there. They'd get Julie back. He had to believe that.

But nothing explained her disappearance.

Once again, his life had been turned upside down.

The most unpredictable thing in his life had come before Julie was in it. His father's sudden heart attack when Luke was twenty-five. One day his dad worked next to him, still pretending he needed guidance in putting together a set of cabinets. The next they were planning his dad's funeral. He looked at the ceiling. He still didn't understand that one.

He worked his jaw. He didn't understand this either. Julie had brought so much stability into his life. A steady calm, as sure as the tides of the river they sometimes went out on with friends. He loved her predictability and steadiness. He loved everything about her.

Swallowing the lump in his throat again, he shifted his weight. At least someone finally listened. The officer had thought he was crazy at first, but it seemed like he would actually look into what had happened to Julie.

He had no idea what would occur next. The coffee cup might help. He couldn't figure out how but clung to hope that it would.

He sucked in air, battling against the pain in his chest. It felt like someone had hammered nails into his heart, piercing him, then plugged up the holes so he couldn't bleed.

Finally, all the customers cleared out. Sue raised her eyebrows, but she didn't ask the question.

He took a deep breath. "We found the cup and think it's hers. Officer...I don't even know his name." Luke shook his head. "Anyway, he's taking the cup back to test it for fingerprints and DNA. At least it convinced him something's off. I'm supposed to get a hair sample from home and meet him at the station."

"Then what? Can I do anything to help?" She fingered the loose yarn in her lap.

He struggled against the urge to scream. He didn't have answers. Helplessness filled him. Meeting the concern in Sue's cobalt eyes, he sighed. "I don't know. Right now, just pray."

"Of course. Keep me updated? You have my number?"

He pulled his cell from his back pocket and scrolled through his contacts. He got to "Mark & Sue." He punched a couple of buttons to make sure he had her number as well as Mark's. "I've got your number. Can you get the Sunday school prayer chain active?" He cleared his throat and swallowed back tears. "You can tell them whatever. Maybe someone will think of something to help. But until we know more, we need prayers most of all."

"OK," Sue whispered. Her gaze moved past Luke to another group coming in, and she forced a smile. "Good morning."

He mouthed thank you to her and headed out.

The twenty-minute drive home seemed much longer. Turning the engine off, he sat in the car, surrounded by silence. The driveway looked barren without Julie's car, even though it'd only been a month since their wedding and her moving in.

She almost always arrived home before him. Even if he got off early, he rarely came home immediately, running errands or stopping by his mom's to allow time for Julie to get there first and enjoy the alone time she craved.

He fought the threatening tears and pounded the steering wheel. He'd almost lost it at the police station. He wouldn't let it happen again. That would mean he'd lost hope. Lost his Julie. That was unacceptable.

He grabbed a sandwich bag from the kitchen on his way to their bathroom. The trash should have been emptied the night before for pickup today, hopefully. His stomach relaxed when he pulled the can out of the cabinet and spotted the hair Julie had pulled from her brush that morning and a couple Q-tips were the only things in it. He slipped the hair in the bag. As he passed back through their bedroom, he grabbed the framed copy of their engagement picture from the wall and one of Julie in her work costume from the bedside table.

Frigid air whirled around him as he dashed back out to his truck. Funny how he hadn't noticed the cold earlier. He shut it out and started the engine. If only he could block out his racing thoughts.

Instead, he focused on what he could do, what else he could tell the officer. He wracked his brain as he drove to the station, hoping he hadn't forgotten anything.

He groaned. He had to call Fran. Julie's mom needed to know. He turned into the station parking lot and pulled into an empty spot. Slipping his phone out of his back pocket, he unlocked it. He scanned to Fran's name and his finger hovered over the call option. He closed his eyes and hit the off button. He'd wait. See what the cop said then call her.

He pushed through the glass door leading into the station. The hum of conversations and phones ringing greeted him. A laugh rang out from an unseen woman. His heart ached. It'd only been a few hours, and he missed Julie's laugh already.

Slowing his gait, he crept up to the clerk's desk. The young officer who'd gotten the brunt of his wrath his first trip to the police station a couple hours earlier met his gaze. "I, um, I'm here to see the officer I spoke with this morning. I didn't get his name."

"Cooper."

"Officer Cooper. Can I see him? He asked me to get some things and meet him back here." He held up the bag of hair and the pictures.

The clerk picked up the phone and punched in some numbers. "He's here."

"I'm sorry," Luke said after he hung up the phone. He held up the picture of Julie in her costume. "This is my wife, Julie. She's missing. How would you feel if it was your wife?"

The clerk's face softened.

"Mr. Montgomery," said a deep voice from behind.

He swiveled to face Officer Cooper. "I brought

some of Julie's hair. And these."

Officer Cooper took the items and handed them to the clerk. "Get the hair to the lab. Scan the pictures, take Mr. Montgomery out of this one, and print a dozen copies of each. Get the originals back to Mr. Montgomery when you get done."

"Luke."

Officer Cooper looked at him. "What?"

"My name's Luke. I hope this won't take long and I don't have to spend a lot of time here, but Mr. Montgomery is too formal. That was my father's name."

Officer Cooper's stern face mellowed for the first time. "Terrence." He stuck his hand out and Luke shook it. "Let's head back to the interview room." He motioned toward the hall they'd gone down earlier that morning.

~*~

Was. Luke had said Mr. Montgomery was his father's name. So he'd lost his dad at some point. At least he'd had one, unlike Terrence. But now the guy had a missing wife. Maybe.

Nothing came up when he ran a background check on Luke Montgomery. He'd lived in Williamsburg his whole life. A few speeding tickets when he was younger. One accident on record. Beyond that, the guy seemed as clean as his wife's car.

He didn't grab coffee this time. He had two bottles of water waiting for them in the room. He plunked into his seat and waited a handful of heartbeats for Luke to do the same. "Have you tried calling Julie again?"

"Once, before I left CW. It went straight to voicemail."

"OK. So we've got to assume her battery's dead or her phone's been turned off."

"Her battery's not dead. She plugs her phone in every night."

Terrence let a grin slip. This lady certainly was habitual.

He grabbed the water bottle, unscrewed the cap, and took a sip. Her consistency most likely meant she liked control in her life, and that might be a clue to something. What, he wasn't sure. "We'll assume it's turned off, then. What's her number? We'll track the last phone calls, texts, and pings off a tower."

He recorded the number Luke rattled off from memory. "OK. What else can you tell me about your wife? Any enemies? Uncommonly friendly customers?"

Luke shook his head. "No. She's the sweetest person I've ever met. A little OCD but sweet. We live a normal life. We go to church, we both have good jobs, and we spend time with friends. That's it."

Terrence held a pen. He clicked it over and over. Normal people. Clean living. It didn't add up to a missing wife. It made no sense for someone to abduct a perfect stranger out in the open, yards from where she worked. His gut told him only someone who knew the victim would do it that way. A stranger would have taken a moment of opportunity, grabbed her from her car. This reeked of planning.

"How about her past? Any old boyfriends?"

"She went out with someone in high school and a little after, but she's never said much about him. There were only a few other dates between him until we got together."

"Did she say how that relationship ended? Was it ugly?"

Luke leaned forward. "No, not that she said. I know she dated someone for a long time. She's never even mentioned his name."

"What about her mother? Would she know more?"

He winced. "Maybe."

"What?"

"I haven't told her Julie's missing yet. I almost called her but wanted to wait. To see if we could find out something first."

Terrence closed his notebook. "I think it's time you called her. Let her know we're heading to her house. She's the best person to talk to next. She'll know about Julie's life before you met."

Luke pulled his phone out and looked at him, hesitating.

He drained his water and stood. "I'm going to go get another. I'll let you make the call in private."

Terrence left the room but stepped through the next door into the observation room instead of walking down the hall. He hit the speaker button. Luke pulled out his phone and dialed slowly.

"Hi, Fran. It's me again." He paused. "I wanted to ask...have you talked to Julie this morning?"

Luke's worry lines on his forehead creased deeper, and his shoulders slumped. "No. I called earlier really to see if you'd heard from her."

He paused again. "She didn't show up at work today." He cleared his throat. "Her car's there. But she's not."

Terrence played with his empty water bottle. Poor guy. He could only imagine what the mother-in-law was saying on her end. Luke swiped at a tear. "I'm at the police station now. Officer Cooper wants to come talk to you." Luke nodded at her response. "We'll be right over." Ending the call, he again lowered his head.

Terrence watched him a minute longer before exiting the observation room. Opening the door, he cleared his throat. "You ready?"

Luke looked up. "Yeah."

"I'll follow you."

They wove through the familiar streets of Williamsburg, taking 199 until it turned into Newman Road. Terrence followed Luke's dark green work truck. It wasn't a newer model, but he'd obviously taken care of it. Both of the Montgomerys drove older cars. The neighborhood they wove through now was not one of the richer in Williamsburg. Everything screamed normal and simple about these people's lives. Looks could be deceiving, though. He'd learned that long ago.

Luke pulled into a driveway, and Terrence pulled

up to the curb. The small ranch house sat back from the road a few yards further than the houses on either side of it. Tan siding with green shutters made it attractive. The front curtains and blinds were open, a salt-and-pepper haired woman paced on the other side. Julie's mother, he assumed. He wondered if she was as squeaky clean as the daughter. This certainly wasn't a neighborhood they had frequent trouble with. He couldn't remember the last time he'd answered a call in this area.

Luke trudged up the drive as Terrence exited his car and clicked the lock button. Before Luke had a chance to knock, the front door swung open. The slight of a woman stepping through it threw her arms around her son-in-law. Her eyes were red and swollen.

Luke let the woman weep on his shoulder. "It's going to be OK, Fran. We'll find her."

He pulled away, stepped back, and motioned towards Terrence. "This is Officer Cooper. He wants to ask you some questions. See if we can figure this thing out."

Terrence stepped forward and held out his hand. Fran's petite hand looked ghostly and miniature next to his muscular, dark one. "I'm sorry to meet you under these circumstances, Ms. Byers."

"Oh, please call me Fran. Thank you so much for coming. For helping."

Her tiny, shaking hand began to warm against his. He liked the brisk weather, but she had no coat on and began to shiver. "Fine. Fran. I'm Terrence. Can we go inside?"

"Sure." She pulled her hand from his and grasped Luke's arm, leaning against him as they entered the house.

Once in the small living room, Fran let go of Luke and straightened her shoulders. Terrence allowed her to take his coat. She coaxed Luke out of his too.

Fran glided back into the living room. "Can I get you a drink? I have freshly brewed coffee. Or I can whip up some hot chocolate or hot tea."

"No, thank you." Terrence eased into the burgundy recliner. Simple furniture, but nice. It fit the house, and what he'd observed of Ms. Byers.

She and Luke sat next to each other on a matching sofa. "Ms....um, Fran, I'm not sure how much Luke has told you."

Watery chestnut eyes glanced up at Luke. She returned her gaze to Terrence. "Just that Julie went to work this morning but didn't show up. It's not like her. She would never leave without telling Luke. Or me. We talk several times a day. She tells me everything. She wouldn't..." Fran let her words run out and her eyes glazed over.

She was remembering something. He waited, studying Fran's face turn from worry to fear. Was it possible she grew paler? She wrung her hands in her lap. There was something she wasn't saying.

"Fran?" Terrence prompted.

She shook herself to the present. "Yes?"

Terrence leaned forward. "What is it? You looked like you remembered something."

She shot to her feet and paced again. "I thought

we were OK after all this time. That he'd forgotten. Or at least given up by now." She looked out the window. "And if he came, I figured he'd come after me. Not her."

Luke popped off the sofa and stood in the way of Fran's pacing. He reached out for her, held each arm in his hands, and examined her face. "Who are you talking about? Who would come after Julie?"

"I didn't know if she ever told you. I'm not even sure how much she remembers." Fran averted her eyes from Luke's piercing gaze and swiped the tears away.

Imploring, his eyes pleaded for an answer. "Who, Fran? Tell me!"

She cringed then sighed. "Her father."

Luke let go and stepped back. His mouth fell open. His eyebrows creased together. "Her father?"

"Yes." Her two tiny hands wrung together. She stopped them and looked up to meet Luke's confused gape. "So, she's said nothing."

"She told me he left when she was eight, and you've never heard from him since."

Her small frame shrank as she hunched her shoulders and dropped her chin down. "The second part is true. We haven't heard from him since Julie was eight."

Luke's face reddened. "And the first? He didn't leave? Julie lied to me?" He tapped his chest. "Why would she lie to me? To me! I've trusted her with everything. And she didn't trust me with this?"

Terrence stood. Luke's anger and distress were understandable. But the focus had gotten off the information he needed. He couldn't afford the only person who possibly held vital information to pass out in front of him. She looked ghostly, weak, and even more frail than when he'd arrived. "Ms. Fran. I think you'd better sit."

He guided her back to the sofa and took the spot next to her. He understood all too well a single mother raising a child by herself. This felt different, though. Something wasn't being said. If Julie Montgomery's mother had reason to suspect her father in Julie's disappearance, he needed to know why.

He steadied his gaze on Luke, who deflated and fell into a chair. He turned to the delicate woman sitting beside him. "Now, Ms. Fran. Tell me about Julie's father."

THREE

A cold chill ran up Fran's spine as visions of her ex-husband raced in. Flashes of brutality, anger, and bitter words assaulted her. She took a deep breath and pushed back the memories. She had to focus on the facts.

She met Officer Cooper's dark eyes. Reserved, but kind. She liked him already. Just as she had liked Luke from the moment she'd met him. Julie had introduced her to Luke at a church picnic, and he'd stolen her heart by talking to her almost more than he'd talked to her daughter.

Her gaze wandered to her son-in-law and met the pain there. What she had to say would most likely bring him more anguish. He'd have to get over his shock and hurt at what she was about to tell and, instead, focus on what had to be done to find Julie.

With no way to avoid revealing secrets, she returned her gaze to Officer Cooper and plunged ahead. "First, I need to tell you that my name hasn't always been Fran Byers. It's my mother's maiden name. I changed mine and Julie's names when I left Stuart."

"You left him? You changed your name?"

She looked over at her son-in-law's contorted face, and her heart ached. How she loved him. "Luke, Julie had her reasons for not telling you. She didn't want you to pity her. Feel sorry for what she'd been through. She simply wanted you to love her for who she is. That's my Julie."

Terrence's solemn voice broke in. "Go on, Ms. Fran. You left your husband and changed your name. Was he abusive?"

She winced. "Before Julie and I became who we are now, we were Frances and Julia Parker. My husband was Stuart Parker. We'd gone to school together our whole lives and started dating when I was sixteen. I got pregnant our senior year of high school. I didn't know until the day he proposed that his father beat him regularly. He'd hid it well."

She paused, recalling the fear that had filled her seventeen-year-old, pregnant self. And the shock of how Stuart looked the day he promised to love her forever. She inhaled deeply. "He brought me his class ring shortly after I found out. He had a black eye and bruised rib and said he didn't care what his father thought. He was going to marry me. And he promised he'd be different from his dad."

Terrence's hand stilled over his notebook, and he looked up. "But he wasn't."

Turning to stare out the window, she counted to ten before answering. "No. He wasn't. That baby came along. My beautiful Rebecca. Money got tighter and tighter, and Stuart became drunker and meaner. I could never do anything right. I kept trying. Kept praying. I thought it was working because he never touched Rebecca. I could take his back hand as long as he didn't hit her."

"She has a sister," Luke whispered.

She stopped fighting the tears and let them roll down her cheeks. "I was seven months pregnant with Julia the first time he smacked Rebecca. She was eight and tried to make dinner one night because I was so sick. The kitchen was a disaster and dinner burnt. He slapped her across the face so hard I couldn't send her to school for almost a week. But now I had another baby on the way. My parents couldn't support us. No one else in town would have taken us in. They all knew Stuart's wrath."

Terrence shifted in his seat. "So you stayed."

She met his gaze. Terrence's dark eyes held no accusation. "I stayed."

Luke cleared his throat. "He hit Julie."

She'd lived with this fact for over two decades. It still stung. He'd need time to let it all sink in. "Things didn't get better after Julia was born. My two beautiful girls in a house of hate. I protected them as much as I could."

"What made you leave?" Terrence asked.

She stood and shuffled over to the window. She swallowed the old fear and turned to face the men waiting expectantly. "Julia was seven. Rebecca, who was fifteen at the time, came home late one night after going to a football game with some friends, and Stuart went ballistic. He dragged her to her room by her hair and locked the door. She screamed for the first ten minutes. Then nothing. He stomped out and started on a second twelve pack. I had hidden in my room with Julia, singing to drown out the noise. After Stuart passed out and Julia went to sleep, I rushed to Rebecca's room, but the door was locked. I begged for her to let me in, but she never answered my pleas. I finally found something to pick the lock and found the room empty. She'd left."

"So you looked for her?" Terrence asked.

She turned her head.

Luke sat riveted, with his elbows on his knees.

"No. I didn't. I figured wherever she was had to be safer than home. That day I began to plan my escape. Mine and Julia's. We left the day she turned eight. Since then her birthday has been a double celebration." She released a breath shakily.

"Ms. Fran, I know this is hard. You've never heard from your husband since that day?"

"No. We lived in Bakersville, in the mountains. I'd saved enough money to get bus tickets to Lynchburg. A women's shelter kept us safe until I could get a job and a small apartment. I legally changed our names while we were at the shelter. I kept a post office box about forty-five minutes away that I used to communicate with my parents. They said Stuart went mad after we left. We'd told no one where we were going, however, so there was no one to get information from."

"But you think he's found you now and taken Julie?"

"He swore he'd find Rebecca after she left. When he didn't, he told me if I ever got it in my head to leave and take Julia, he'd hunt us down and get back what was his if it was the last thing he did." She looked steadily at Terrence, ignoring the quivering inside. "My husband did not make idle threats."

~*~

Luke stood. He couldn't sit a moment longer. This man, Julie's father, was out there somewhere. He'd beat her. Julie had never said a word. Never let slip that she'd had a bad day in her life. Only that her dad had left, and she and her mom had moved a couple times. And now he'd come back in some perverted sense of getting what was stolen from him years ago.

Fran was tiny. She might be one-ten soaking wet. He couldn't imagine her taking the brunt of an abusive husband. He wondered that she hadn't completely broken, both physically and emotionally.

A vision of Julie's own small frame getting hit assailed him. "I need air." He covered the room in three steps and headed out the door without his coat. Cold air blasted his face and wind ripped through his cotton shirt. Why in the world hadn't she told him? She should have trusted him with everything. With this most of all. It was his job to protect her, but he couldn't keep her safe from what he didn't know.

He studied his mother-in-law and Officer Cooper through the large front window. He didn't understand how they could just sit there talking about Julie being abused at the hand of her father. Weight of the new knowledge pressed on his chest. He fought to breathe. Struggled to understand. Every fiber of his being longed to go find Stuart Parker and give him the same treatment he'd given his family.

But that wouldn't help him find Julie.

What could he do? Nothing.

But he couldn't stand here doing nothing either. He had to get out of here.

He stormed to his truck, flung the door open, grabbed his tennis shoes from under the front seat of his truck, and shoved his feet into them after unlacing and discarding his work boots. He couldn't run away from the facts that his wife was missing and had kept secrets from him, dangerous secrets, but he could pound out his frustration on a few miles of pavement. Anything was better than helplessly loitering in the driveway.

~*~

Terrence accepted the cup of black coffee from Ms. Fran. He sipped from the mug and stared out the front window as Luke tore down the street in a sprint. This guy's life had been invaded and flipped upside down in the last few hours. He shook his head.

The squeaky clean image of the missing woman he was getting to know by the people and things in her life had gotten a big smudge, but not due to anything she had done.

Ms. Fran had done everything right. She'd left, changed their names, and moved a second time. The names could have been changed a little more, and they could have gone out of state, but still. He couldn't see why her ex-husband would have picked this time to kidnap Julie.

He sipped the piping hot liquid again and grinned. Not quite police-grade, but he didn't envision Ms. Fran making a strong, bold brew. He peeked at her cup. There had to be almost as much milk as coffee, and he'd bet more than one teaspoon of sugar.

"Coffee OK?"

"It's fine. How are you?"

Her eyes clouded over. "Scared for my daughter. I know what Stuart's capable of."

"You're sure it's him? There's no one else who might put your daughter in danger?" He glanced out the window. "There aren't any problems in any relationships in Julie's life?"

"I'm sure. Who else could it be?" Fran followed his gaze to the truck in the driveway. "Not Luke. He adores Julie. He'd only get violent if she were threatened by someone else."

"I think I saw a taste of that this morning when he first came to the police station."

"No, Luke has been one of the best things in our

lives. And he's worried sick."

He seemed to be. But Terrence had witnessed people put on great acts before. Shown the world what they wanted everyone to see.

He filed those thoughts away and returned to his previous ones. "Why do you think your ex-husband acted now? Has something happened that would have tipped him off? Caused him to make a move after all this time?"

Fran gazed toward the hallway. She rose and motioned him to follow. She led him to a small, simply decorated bedroom. Julie's wedding picture adorned the left wall.

"Julie and Luke got married only a month ago. She put an announcement in the paper." Reaching a hand up and resting it on the picture of her daughter's beautiful face, Fran spoke softly. "We talked about whether it would be a good idea. She wanted to be normal. Putting a wedding announcement in the paper was normal. Her friends and Luke's family expected it. I thought..." She choked back a sob. "I thought it would be OK. So much time had passed. It was just a local paper."

So anyone who wanted to know where to find her would have no problem after that. Terrence turned to Ms. Fran and directed her back to the living room before she lost herself in rehashing decisions. "Now I'm going to need you to tell me everything you can remember about your husband and his family."

A half hour later, Terrence closed his notebook. He enjoyed talking with Ms. Fran. Even talking about a tragic past, she revealed her strength and will to survive. He wished he could have gotten to know her under different circumstances. She reminded him of his own mother. Single. Small in stature but strong in spirit.

The front door opened and Luke strode in, covered in sweat and heaving to catch his breath.

Terrence accepted his coat from Ms. Fran and slid his arms into the sleeves. He pulled out two business cards. "I have enough to get started. Call me if you think of anything else." He looked at Luke. "Or have any questions."

Luke accepted the card. "Thanks."

Fran squeezed his arm. "Thank you, Terrence. Please bring our Julie home. She means the world to us." Before he stepped through the door, she turned, wrapped an arm around Luke, and pulled him back into the living room.

There was nothing he could do about Luke's distress over his wife's deception. However, he could do something about finding her. He let himself out the front door and walked with purpose to his car. He had a missing woman to find.

~*~

Luke dropped onto the sofa and buried his face in his hands. Fran wrapped her arm around his back. His heart rate slowed as he sat soaking in her comfort.

After several minutes had passed, he released a shuddering sigh. "Why didn't she tell me, Fran? Why didn't she trust me with this?"

"I don't know, Luke. I encouraged her to tell you. I never asked if she did."

"What else don't I know?" He searched his mother-in-law's face for revelations of any further secrets. Her brow crinkled in anguish and her eyes were wide with fretfulness.

"Nothing that I know of. But you know Julie. She tells what she wants to tell. She's always been a private person."

"Private is one thing. I'm her husband. I thought we'd shared everything."

Fran actually laughed. "Luke, you've only known each other three years. You've only been married a month. You've have only scraped the surface of getting to know each other."

He dropped his head. How could he have missed so much?

Leaning close to his ear, Fran whispered, "You know the most important things, Luke. Julie loves you. She loves God. And she loves the life you have together. Don't forget that."

He did know those things. But the events of this morning had rocked everything he thought he knew. He had to consider the possibility that she had disappeared out of choice. Perhaps she decided she didn't love him. Maybe she was afraid he'd change like her father had. He could no longer guess at what she might be thinking.

"Luke."

He met Fran's gaze.

"Julie loves you, and we're going to find her. Terrence seems very nice and not a cop who'll take this lightly."

"Yeah." Discouragement and weariness weighed him down. He'd left the anger in little bits along the path he'd run. The confusion remained.

"Go take a shower. Your extra clothes are in the spare bedroom closet. Julie even has some things in the dresser that belong to you in case y'all ever had an impromptu sleep-over."

His wife. Always thinking ahead. Being prepared for anything. Now he knew a little bit more why.

But he didn't know whether she'd held even more secrets from him.

FOUR

Terrence punched the familiar numbers into his phone. It rang twice before someone picked up. "Lab."

"Cooper, here. Did you get the results from the coffee cup, prints, and hair sample I gave you?"

"Yeah, I've got some of it here." Paper rustled in the pause. "OK, two sets of prints showed up. One matches the set you gave me. My guess is the second set will match some café clerk."

He scribbled a note. "Right. I'll call the husband to see where she stopped for coffee and go by there to find out who served her. What about the lipstick stain?"

"There was enough there to get a good sample, but we're still waiting for the preliminary results. You know how long this stuff takes."

Nothing helpful. DNA testing would take longer. Too long. "All right. Text me as soon as you get the prelim results in. When do you expect them?"

"Backup's not too bad right now. Tomorrow at best. Thursday at worst."

He drummed his fingers on his desk, swallowing impatience. "Thanks."

Hanging up and leaning back in his chair, he mulled over the case in front of him. He debated whether it really was a case. His experience and gut said yes. But no hard evidence had shown up. However, nothing else pressed for his attention, and his instincts tended to be spot on.

Game plan time. He'd follow up on the coffee clerk after lunch. First, though, he'd track down Stuart Parker. Terrence's only suspect looked good for being responsible. A possessive, abusive father feeling robbed of his family. One wedding announcement in the paper and a cover that had worked for almost twenty years was blown in an instant.

His phone rang. He picked it up. "Cooper."

"Hey, hon. Just wondering how your day's going."

An automatic smile took over Terrence's face. "Hey, Ma. Busy. How 'bout you?"

"Good. Baking up a fresh batch of peanut butter cookies."

His nose tingled and stomach rumbled. "Sounds good. I may have to come by later."

Her laugh rang across the line. "I thought you might feel that way. Why not come by tomorrow? Have dinner, top it off with some cookies, and go caroling with me."

He swallowed a groan. "Don't know if I'll have time, Ma. I have a new case that may take me out of town for a couple days."

"OK." Her voice came over less enthusiastic. "Then come by on your way out of town, and I'll have a goody bag for you."

"Thanks. I'll buzz you before heading over."

"OK, sweetie. I'll let you get back to work."

He hung up. His ma was the bright light of his life. Even if she did constantly harass him about getting more involved at church and settling down with a nice, Christian girl.

He tapped his pen on the open pad in front of him. What would it have been like if he'd seen his ma get beaten when he a kid? How would he have reacted?

He'd have probably killed the man, father or not. His mother had never talked about his dad. Whenever he'd asked, she would redirect, saying his heavenly Father loved them and that was enough. For the first time in his life, he thought it possible that growing up without a father wasn't the worst thing he could have experienced.

Shoving his thoughts aside, he brought his computer screen to life. He clicked and typed his way to the right database and entered the information he'd gotten from Ms. Fran. Parker, Stuart; Bakersville, VA; 1961.

He tapped his pen on the desk as he waited for the search results. It didn't take long. He leaned in and clicked his way through the links.

Stuart Parker had been arrested for assault and battery in Bland County in 1994. That would have been a year after Fran and Julie left. Then he had a string of DUIs. Bland County in 1997 and 1999. Then one in

Pulaski in 2000. A deeper look into the records showed he did a six-month stint in jail. He hadn't had another blemish on his record since and completed his probation two years before. His current address showed he lived in Loudoun County. Terrence recorded the street and house number.

Northern Virginia sure was a far cry from deep in the Appalachian Mountains.

He continued to dig. Parker had moved after getting off probation. Parker seemed to have avoided any further criminal charges in over a decade, not so much as a parking ticket. His address also showed a Pauline Parker. A new wife.

The woman was either very foolish or didn't have a clue about her husband's past.

He closed the window and turned to the next task on the mental list he'd created. He flipped through his notebook. Then he stopped and dialed the number by Luke's name.

"Hello?"

"It's Officer Cooper. I haven't found much yet, but I have a question for you."

"OK."

"We got two sets of prints off the coffee cup. One matched the boy who found it. The other, we suspect, belongs to the clerk who sold it to Mrs. Montgomery. Do you know what Starbucks she visits?"

"Yeah. The one on Mooretown Road."

"Thanks."

"So it matched? The cup's hers?"

Terrence closed his notebook. "I don't know. We

haven't had enough time to get the DNA results. But I thought I'd try to get a match on the second set of prints."

"Then what?" Luke's voice was gravelly. The man had to be exhausted.

And they'd only begun. "I've found the current information plus some background on her father. I'm going to drive up there tonight."

"Up there? Where is he?"

"Luke, I can't answer that. I know you're going stir crazy and want to do something, but let me handle this. It's my job."

He sighed. "OK."

"I'll call you as soon as there's an update." Surprisingly, he meant it. This case felt different somehow. Terrence shook off the feeling.

"Just find her." Desperation laced the man's request.

He hung up the phone and strode to the captain's office. He knocked on the slightly ajar door.

Captain Ross lifted his shiny bald head, his attention leaving the folder lying open on the desk. "Yes, Officer Cooper?"

"I have a new case, I think."

Ross raised his brows.

Clearing his throat, Terrence plunged ahead, describing Luke Montgomery's visit first thing that morning and everything he'd discovered thus far. "So, the dad is the only probable suspect, but he's up in Northern Virginia."

"Your desk clear?"

"Yes, sir. Well, other than a bit of paperwork."

Ross tapped on his keyboard, inspecting the contents of the screen. He clicked the mouse a few times before looking up. "I don't see anything too pressing that's not being taken care of by someone else. How long do you expect to be gone?"

"Overnight at most."

Ross rubbed his hand over his smooth scalp. "I think you have something worth checking into."

"Thanks, sir. I'll call you first thing tomorrow with an update." He turned to leave.

"Cooper."

He stopped and looked at his boss. "Sir?"

"Take someone with you."

"Yes, sir."

Great. He'd have to take along some rookie who needed hand-holding. Most everyone else worked active cases.

He sauntered over to his desk and examined the buzzing activity in the room. He grinned and hollered over a couple rows. "Hey, Patterson."

"Yo."

"Don't you have a brother who's a deputy in Loudoun County?"

"Yeah. Carl. Why?"

"You got anything going on today?"

Patterson shoved some paperwork aside. "Nope."

Terrence laughed. "Been in the 'burg too long?"

"Too long since I've seen Carl." Patterson ambled over to his desk. "Besides, I'm curious to know what's got ya traveling."

He grabbed his notebook. "I'll fill you in on the way. How 'bout a stop at Starbucks first?"

"Sure. You paying?" Patterson chuckled as he pulled on his coat.

"We'll stop by my mother's place. She's been baking. Food for the road." Terrence offered.

"No objection." Patterson followed Terrence out of the station.

~*~

The stop at the coffee shop proved productive. Terrence talked to the clerk who remembered Julie coming by that morning. "Tall nonfat latte. Same as every morning."

He obtained the clerk's fingerprints to compare to the ones on the cup. "Thanks. We'll contact you if we have any more questions."

Terrence nibbled from the care package he'd picked up from his mom and filled Patterson in on the morning and the case as they headed west on I-64, then north on I-95. Patterson called his brother, who said to come by the station and they'd ride together to Parker's house. Carl called back after an hour and confirmed what Terrence had found. Stuart Parker had been living clean since moving to Loudoun County. Or, at least, he hadn't been caught.

Traffic thickened around Fredericksburg and stayed steady all the way to Northern Virginia. At least they weren't travelling during rush hour. It'd have taken them an extra hour or two had they left much later. As it was, they planned to meet Carl at four.

~*~

Luke checked his caller ID and considered ignoring it. This was the last thing he needed. "I'll be right back." He squeezed Fran's hand and walked to the kitchen. "Hello."

"Hey, handsome. How are you?"

"OK, what's up?"

"Not much. Just wanted to know if my favorite sweetie had enough time to take a long break and join me for lunch today. I haven't seen you in ages."

"Mom, I came over twice last week. The dryer wasn't really broken just clogged with lint. And the front door simply needed some WD-40."

"Well, what's a mom to do? I don't have anyone else to look after me. Can't you spare an hour? I'm fixing Ruebens."

Of course, she'd fixed his favorite sandwich. "Not today."

"What's wrong? Are you meeting her for lunch? She gets to see you every night."

Luke envisioned the pout his mother had perfected. She had been needy and hovering before his dad passed away. Since then, she'd been downright overbearing. "Mom, it's not that."

"Then what? What could be so important to keep you away from your mother? The person who loves you most in this world."

He leaned against the counter, laying his head on the cabinet above. "Julie's missing."

"Julie's missing? You mean she left and broke your heart like I said she would. I told you–"

"Don't start, Mother. Julie's a good woman and a good wife. She's disappeared, and it looks like she's been…" He choked on the word. He hadn't said it yet. Speaking the words out loud made the whole thing all too real. "Kidnapped. She's been taken by someone."

"Then I'm sure she did something to provoke whoever it was. She's arrogant, flaunting her stuff everywhere."

"Mother, stop it. You have never given Julie a chance or tried to get to know her. And if that's how you're going to talk about my wife, you can do it elsewhere. I won't listen to it anymore." He ended the call and felt better than he had all day. At least he could do something for Julie. Even if it was to defend her against his own mother.

"Your mom?" Fran's soft voice startled him.

He pushed off the counter and winced. "You heard?"

"Yeah." Her grin matched her gentle voice. "It's no secret your mother is not a fan of my daughter."

"It's not Julie, really. She wouldn't have approved of anyone. I'm her darling son."

"I know. It's her main redeeming quality."

He fell into a chair and plucked a grape out of the

bowl in the middle of the table.

"You hungry?"

"I shouldn't be. Not while Julie's missing. I feel so helpless."

"But you did run a few miles this morning. And I'd be willing to wager you didn't eat the snack Julie packed for your morning break."

He cocked his head to the side. "She is predictable, isn't she?"

"Very."

"Is that because of the past? Her father?"

She sank into a chair and covered his hands with hers. "I don't know. Maybe. Things were so chaotic when we lived with him. We never knew what to expect when he came home. Then Rebecca disappeared. Life had no normal. No steady. And I'm sure as a little girl, Julie felt completely out of control." She sighed. "When we lived in the shelter, we had routine. We ate at the same time every day. She went to school regularly. The same program ran the same day each week. Life became normal. I guess Julie clung to that."

"I love her normal, Fran. Her predictability." He hung his head. "I don't know what I'll do without her."

She laid a hand on his shoulder. "Don't think that way, Luke. We'll get her back."

"I hope so." His phone buzzed, and he jumped. A text from Sue. He read it aloud. "Contacted everyone. Will bring dinner to Fran's at six. Will pray after we eat."

Fran's lips turned up in a smile that didn't reach her eyes. "Julie has good friends."

"Yes, she does."

"And even better, she has a great God. He knows exactly where she is and what she's facing."

His mind spun and heat seared every thought. Why had God allowed this to happen? It didn't mesh with the God he worshipped every Sunday. The God who was supposed to protect them and keep them safe.

He met her gaze.

"Our instincts usually have us act first then pray when things don't go well. Why don't we try praying first and trust God to show us if and how we need to act?"

His heart ached and mind spun. The misery burned its way down as he swallowed. He didn't want to pray. He wanted God to help them find Julie. Have her show up just as quickly as she'd disappeared.

Fran grasped his hands in hers. "Luke?"

His nose burned, and his eyes moistened. He nodded.

She bowed her head. "Dear Lord. Our most gracious heavenly Father. We come to You humble and desperate. Our precious Julie is missing from our sight. But we know she's not hidden from Yours. We lift her up for protection, strength, and ask for wisdom for both of us and Officer Cooper. Amen."

Fran was right, but he longed to hold Julie in his arms. He wanted answers. So far, God hadn't offered any.

FIVE

Julie peeled her eyes open. Light battered them, and she slammed them shut. Her head pounded and her tongue stuck to the roof of her mouth. She moved it around, trying to pull out some moisture. Her throat stung.

She couldn't move her arms. Or her legs.

Bile rose in her throat. As she squirmed, she met resistance. The scratchy strings of a thick rope rubbed against her wrists and ankles. The layers of her skirting sat heavy on her legs. At least she was covered as she lay sprawled out like a pig on a barbeque.

Tears wet her eyes, and she opened them to slits. The light turned the volume up on the throbbing in her skull, but she refused to retreat back into the dimness behind her lids. Her limbs were each bound to their own bed post. Nothing looked familiar. Where was she?

His face came to the forefront of her mind. She replayed what had happened, trying to figure out why and what she'd done wrong to make herself vulnerable again.

He'd been standing outside her building at work. Her heart had paused a few beats when he opened his coat to reveal the black pistol held in his left hand. Her body shook as it had in that moment.

He'd walked her to his car, gun pressed into her side under his coat. She had sat stunned in the passenger seat, flinching when he closed his door and hit the lock button.

"What do you want?" she'd asked.

He smiled, pulled out a thick scarf, and used it to cover his mouth and nose. Then he set the gun in his lap and waved a vial under her nose. The sweet, rubbing alcohol smell assaulted her nostrils as her head swam. She turned away, and he started the engine. Her vision blurred and mind dulled as she struggled to focus on the familiar buildings whizzing by.

"What...do you want?"

His laugh rebounded throughout the car, bouncing off the windows. "Only what's mine."

A shiver ran up her spine, and her head spun. Why now? A tear slipped down her cheek, and she laid her head on the window. She had prayed, her eyes closing with heavy weariness.

Now, she found herself strapped to a bed. A nightmare. A horrible, living nightmare.

She peeled her eyes open again and looked around the room. How much time had passed? Had she dozed for mere moments or fallen into a deep sleep for a few hours?

A movement caught her attention. She recognized

the figure when he passed by the door. The disheveled hair, the shirt sleeves rolled up to expose over-exercised arms.

Oh, God. Let this not be true. Get me out of here. I can't live through this again. Help me.

Tears streamed down her face.

"Good afternoon, sunshine."

The arrogance and intrusiveness of his voice turned her stomach like the smell of putrid meat. He must find joy in her helplessness and tears. She refused to look at him.

"Aw, come on. Don't be like that. I come bringing food. You must be hungry by now."

She remained silent and still.

"It's your favorite. Chicken soup. Perfect for a cold day like today."

The soup's aroma drifted to Julie's nostrils but brought with it the stench of him. The fact that it was most likely hours past lunch time didn't change her body's reaction. A wave of nausea rose in her throat. Turning her head, she fought the repulsion.

"No? Not hungry yet. Hmm. OK, let's talk."

The tears continued to stream despite her determination to quit. She wouldn't listen to anything he had to say. She didn't have to hear his words.

Oh, God, where are You?

Be strong and brave. Do not be terrified. Do not lose hope. I am the Lord your God. I will be with you everywhere you go.

Julie startled. She didn't recall having ever read those exact words. But as the deepest part of her soul warmed, she had no doubt they came straight from the Lord.

She repeated the words in her mind, and they flowed over her like water from a hot shower first thing in the morning, waking her up. The stream of tears slowed as she meditated on the divine message.

On the third time through, the words got stuck, and the last part faded. Her throat tightened as if a vice had clamped it shut. She was neither strong nor brave.

The battle between her fear and God's words raged in her stomach, and every arrow pierced its lining. She took a deep breath

I will be with you everywhere you go.

She exhaled. God had been with her over the last few years when things were good. God still claimed He was with her where she was, facing who she was. She'd simply have to cling to that.

A bowl crashed to her left. Julie popped her eyes open. They met the fury in his.

"You will not ignore me," he spewed. "You belong to me. Answer me." He moved to within inches of her face. "I'll give you a little time to adjust and think about it, but don't forget. I know how to make you listen."

The memories flooded her mind, causing a shudder to rise up her spine. OK, God. You said You're here. I will not lose hope, but I'm going to need You every second. I can't live through this again.

The door slammed, and she sighed with relief. She tried to shift her position, desiring to lay on her side, but her movement was extremely limited. There had to be a way out. Scanning the room, she began filing away everything she saw.

She assumed the door through which he'd swept in and stormed out led to the rest of the house. Two other doors stood close to each other on the wall to her right. The open one led to a bathroom. The other was closed. She guessed it to be a closet. The headboard sat between two windows. She couldn't see anything but trees beyond them. He must have taken her to a cabin in the woods somewhere. Was the cottage five miles or two hundred from her home?

The last wall, the one on her left, held an old wooden dresser, the top of it bare. Nothing in the room felt personal. No pictures. No trinkets. No memorabilia. It seemed no one lived there.

The longer she lay in the room the colder she got. Her gloves had been removed and her fingers had stiffened in the chilled air. She moved her thumb on her left hand, checking for her wedding band. She met only skin, not the newly familiar metal. Tears assaulted her eyes again.

No. She wouldn't give in. Her wedding ring was only a symbol. She was still very much Luke's wife.

Luke. Did he know she was missing yet? Surely, he did. Sue would have called as soon as Julie didn't show up for work on time. They always teased her, saying she needed to loosen up, not be so obsessive about time. She couldn't stand being late, though. Perhaps that had worked in her favor.

Hope soared.

Luke had to know something had happened. He'd

go to the police, and they would be looking for her by now.

But they had no hint to her whereabouts. He was too smart to leave clues. Besides, Luke was oblivious about him. Nothing would lead them to look into him. Unless her mother…She sighed as hopelessness filled her.

She would not give up. The Lord had spoken to her, and she would continue to call out to Him. She moistened her mouth as much as she could and squeaked out the words, "God, You're the only one who knows where I am. Show them. They'll never find me without You. But thank You for reminding me that someone's out there to look for me."

She closed her eyes against another wave of nausea. Maybe it hadn't been the aroma of the soup or his familiar, woody cologne. The chemical he'd used to knock her out might be to blame. Her stomach settled a bit after she took a few deep breaths, and she focused on another pungent smell in the air. Was that smoke from burning wood?

She examined the room again. From her vantage point, no air vents were visible and no air blew.

A wood stove or fire place. That's how the house was heated. She shivered. As long as she found herself stuck in the bedroom with the door closed, she'd freeze. Should she wait until he calmed down and came back on his own? Should she risk calling him back? At least then heat could come in with him and penetrate the stark coldness of the room.

~*~

Carl looked over the hood at Terrence and shut the car door. "I'll take the lead. You jump in whenever you're ready. It's your case, and you know it better."

Terrence preferred to start the questioning, but Carl had been generous enough to meet them and be the intermediary between departments. He'd respect the man's authority in his own district. It wouldn't hurt to let him take the lead. For a few minutes, anyway.

The modest home surprised Terrence. He'd expected Stuart Parker to live in a beaten down section of the area, complete with broken down cars and dilapidated houses. Instead, as they'd woven through the neighborhood, he'd been greeted by small, manicured lawns and a bright playground. Terrence and Patterson hung back as Carl rang the doorbell.

Piano music filtered through the green door. Scales. A muffled, "I'm coming," came a moment before the piano stilled. Heels clicking on the floor preceded the door opening to a small framed woman with shoulder-length brown hair. She glanced from uniform to uniform, and her wide smile froze. "Can I help you?"

Carl stepped forward. "Mrs. Parker?"

The brunette head bobbed.

"We're looking for your husband, Stuart Parker?"

"He's not here." A small girl, Terrence guessed to be about six, raced up behind Mrs. Parker and wrapped her arms around the woman's legs. "Hi, Sweetie. Mommy will be done in a minute. Why don't you go tell Darlene she's done with piano practice and can go play?" The little girl took off and disappeared as fast as she'd emerged.

Carl's voice remained steady. "Your daughter?"

"Yes, Emma. She's five. She's Stuart's. Darlene, my other daughter, is twelve." The smile returned. "Stuart's in the process of adopting her."

Terrence raised his eyebrows and glanced at Patterson. The woman looked sane, but, obviously, her well-kept appearance and perfectly manicured nails hid her madness. Otherwise, she wouldn't even consider letting a man like Stuart Parker adopt her child.

Carl spoke again. "Ma'am, we have a few questions we'd like to ask you about your husband. Do you mind if we come in?"

The calmness plastered on Mrs. Parker's face faltered, her brows scrunching together. She stepped back and opened the door. "Sure."

The three men followed her to a formal living room. The source of the music previously being played stood in a corner.

Mrs. Parker had regained control, the warm smile returning. The only sign of concern she exhibited was the twisting of her wedding band between her right thumb and middle finger. "Please have a seat. May I get you something to drink? Tea, lemonade, coffee?"

Carl eased down into a wooden rocking chair. "No, thank you."

Patterson and Terrence took seats on the opposite ends of a blue plaid sofa. "Coffee," Terrence replied. It looked like the day would be much longer than he'd planned.

"Me, too." Patterson must have come to the same conclusion.

Mrs. Parker nodded and stepped out.

"So?"

Terrence met Carl's gaze. "I don't know. Not what I expected."

Carl eyed the family portraits on the wall. "Me either. Sure you have the right Stuart Parker?"

His gaze stopped on one picture. Older, cleaned up, but the man in the picture was the same one he'd seen on the record he'd looked up. "I'm sure."

"What do you think?"

"I don't know. A new wife, a new life. Holding it in until something sets him off?"

"Here we go." Mrs. Parker glided back into the room holding a tray with a carafe, coffee cups, cream, and an assortment of sweeteners. She turned toward Terrence. "Cream? Sugar?"

"No, black is fine."

She handed him a freshly poured cup, then looked at Patterson.

He answered the unspoken question. "Two sugars. No cream."

Mrs. Parker perched tall and straight in a high-backed beige chair by the piano, facing the three officers. She held her hands in her lap, her fingers again spinning her wedding rings. "OK, what is it I can help you with?"

"Mrs. Parker, we have some questions about your husband."

"Please call me Pauline. What questions do you have?"

Carl glimpsed at Terrence then dove in. "We've come across some information about your husband's past."

Terrence studied her face closely. Pauline showed no surprise. On the contrary, she relaxed her shoulders and leaned back against the chair. "Sir, I'm well aware of my husband's past. We met in AA and haven't had any secrets from the beginning."

Terrence controlled himself and kept his eyes from rolling. How naive women were. Men always had secrets. There was no way Pauline knew the full extent of her husband's history and chose to live in his house with her daughters. If she bought whatever line he'd sold her, she'd also be willing to cover for him and possibly warn him of their coming. Time to take over.

"Ma'am. We'd really like to talk with your husband about some things that have come up recently. I'm sure it's nothing. We simply want to un-muddy the water. Could you tell us where he is?"

"Of course. He's on a skiing trip with a friend. They're at Massanutten."

Terrence pulled his notebook out. "When did he leave?"

"This morning early. I'm not sure what time. I was still in bed." Pauline Parker squinted up at the ceiling. "Umm, before five-thirty. That's when I woke Darlene up for school."

Patterson's and Carl's glances told Terrence they concurred with his thoughts. Plenty of time to make it to Williamsburg if he left before four.

"Could you give us the information for where he's staying? We'd like to clear things up as soon as possible."

"Sure."

Pauline didn't even blink. She must truly trust him. Terrence recorded the information she relayed.

"Thank you, ma'am. We're sorry to interrupt your day but appreciate your help." He asked a few more questions and then determined she had no additional information to help them. He set the empty coffee cup on the tray and stood.

"Of course." Pauline walked them to the door. They'd made it down the three steps when she stopped them. "Um, sir?"

Terrence turned. "Yes?"

Her forehead creased. "This isn't about Rebecca, is it? Has something happened?"

Interesting. "No, ma'am. It has nothing to do with Rebecca."

Her face relaxed. "OK. Thank you." She closed the door.

So she knew about Rebecca. Maybe they should follow up on locating her as well. But first, to track down Stuart Parker, who supposedly had taken a trip to Massanutten. He checked his watch. Almost five o'clock. They could drop Carl back at his headquarters, grab something to eat in a drive-thru, and be at the ski resort by seven.

SIX

Luke stepped out of the shower in Fran's guest bathroom. He cut the fan off and laughter filtered into the room. He didn't know how he could face his friends–their friends. Then again, he didn't know how he'd face the night without them. The first night he'd spend without Julie in a month. Even before they got married, they'd talked every day. The evening loomed long and dark.

Dressed and clean, he reached for the doorknob. His hand refused to turn it. His heart ached. Actually ached. If only he had something to tell them. If Officer Cooper had called with information. Something. Anything. Instead, he'd have to walk into Fran's kitchen and face the three couples he and Julie were closest to with a big fat zero.

He sighed, listening to the hum of familiar voices. They loved him. They would embrace him, not push him. A tired smile broke through. Sue had insisted on bringing dinner. She'd recruited Craig, Heather, Paul, and Dawn to supply drinks and dessert. They'd even hired a babysitter to watch all the kids.

Would he ever get Julie back so they could have children of their own?

A knock on the door brought his head up.

A muffled voice called through the door. "Yo, man. You turnin' into a prune or what?"

Mark. He should have known his best friend wouldn't leave him to wallow in his loneliness. Luke opened the door.

"'Bout time. Sue brought her homemade lasagna, garlic knots, and Dawn brought Tiramisu. My stomach's about ready to jump out and go eat without my assistance."

Luke inhaled. "Smells good."

Mark clasped his shoulder. "Wait 'til you get downstairs." He paused, examining Luke. "How ya holding up?"

"Been running a lot."

"Mmm. Keeping busy. Guess that's better than other options."

"There are other options?"

Mark laughed. "Yeah. But most of them aren't good. I can take you to the gym for a good round in the boxing ring if you need something different."

"I'll let you know."

Mark nodded, squeezed his shoulder, then turned. Luke followed him down the hall into the now full kitchen. The women paused from their dinner preparations when he entered the room and each wrapped him in a warm hug. His stomach growled and he turned. Someone had added a couple of leaves in Fran's table to make room for eight. A pan of steaming lasagna and a basket of bread sat waiting.

Fran touched his arm. "Tea?"

"Sure. Thanks."

He sat in his usual chair, and Fran set a glass of sweet iced tea by his plate. Everyone else chose a seat. Hands joined around the table, heads bowed, and Paul began to pray. "Father, we come grateful for the friends we have around this table. We also come with heavy hearts as one great friend is missing."

A lump formed in Luke's throat.

"We lift our sister Julie up to you. Keep her safe, Lord, and let her know we are here, gathered together for her. Let her know she's not alone. Protect her and bring her home to us safely. Thank You for Your love and thank You for this wonderful food we're about to eat. Amen."

Everyone filled their plates with layers of cheese, noodles and sauce. The lack of conversation hit Luke hard. Unasked questions hung heavily in the air.

He tackled the unspoken questions head on. "I haven't heard anything. I don't have a clue what happened to Julie or why."

Dawn spoke up. "Luke, we don't expect you to have answers. We don't need answers. We love her, too." She looked down at her plate. "We're scared, too."

"I feel like I should be doing something." His voice came out thick.

"Of course you do. All of us do." Mark's eyebrows furrowed. He looked as angry as Luke felt. "That's why we're here. We're praying for Julie. That's what we can do."

Luke sat back. Having friends around was better than pacing, running, and wondering with no distraction. Their presence didn't answer the questions, though. Didn't cause Julie to miraculously reappear. But they did provide a level of comfort. "Thanks."

Heather offered Luke a soft, sympathetic grin. She took a deep breath and turned to Sue. "So, when do you find out the baby's gender?"

Luke picked up his fork. He shouldn't be hungry, but his stomach complained loudly about his third run of the day. His friends talked, shared, and distracted him. He shoveled the first forkful in. Focusing on the food and his friends were the only things keeping him from going crazy or falling apart completely.

~*~

Terrence followed the mechanically voiced instructions and turned off the interstate at the next exit. Less than twenty minutes from Massanutten.

"How many miles you plan on claiming for reimbursement this month?" Patterson asked.

Terrence laughed. "Didn't have it planned, but now that you mention it, we'll have to ask the GPS to take us home the long way."

"If we get to go home tonight. What do you think the chances are we'll actually find Stuart Parker where he told his wife he'd be?"

"I'm not sure." Terrence shook his head. "It could be a cover. Get Julie and take her to a secluded ski resort. Tell the wife he's skiing with a buddy for a few days."

"Then what?"

"Not sure. He's abusive, passionate. He may have made the decision on a whim. Seen the wedding announcement, lost it, and went over the edge. He planned enough to snatch Julie and get her somewhere but not beyond that. You know abusers. They don't think that far ahead."

Patterson drummed his fingers together. "But why the daughter? Why not the wife?"

"He has a new wife now."

"He has a new daughter, too."

Terrence followed the instructions and turned left. "True. None of this has turned out as simple as it first looked."

"Yeah. You thought you just had a bored housewife to find."

Terrence snickered. "My instincts are usually better than that."

"I certainly hope they get better."

He steered onto a gravel lane. "Hmm. Not exactly part of the resort."

"Secluded cabin instead of the more populated hotel or condos."

"I noticed." The rocky drive ended at a log cabin. Smoke curled out of the chimney. A white four-door sedan was parked beside the house. Terrence pulled up behind it and checked the license plate against his notes. "It's Parker's car."

Patterson turned toward him. "How do you want to play this? Think we should call in backup?"

He tapped his notebook. The wife had seemed calm. She had no concerns with giving them Stuart's location. The car matched his records, so she hadn't called to warn him they were coming. He could be lying in wait, but that wouldn't match everything else they'd discovered. "No, I don't think so. We have the element of surprise on our side."

"And there are two of us. Twice as many as you're used to working with."

He shot Patterson a sideways glance. Not the first time he'd been harassed about liking to work alone, just the first time that day. "I'd say let's play it casual. If my instincts are back on track, there's no danger here. If Parker took Julie, she's not here with him."

"OK. I'll follow your lead."

They exited the car and swung the doors shut gently. After crossing the gravel walkway, Terrence knocked on the door. A few seconds later a tall, lanky man with graying hair answered the door. He looked at Terrence, taking in his uniform, eyebrows raised. "Hello? May I help you?"

Parker could have lied to his wife and just his buddy had gone skiing. This guy was in for a rude interruption to his vacation. "We're looking for Mr. Stuart Parker."

He glanced over his shoulder. "Yeah, he's here." He stepped back. "Come on in, officers. He's taking a shower."

That wasn't at all what Terrence expected. The guy was actually there.

Terrence glanced at Patterson then stepped into the open cabin. The room they entered served as a kitchen, dining area, and den. The furniture all seemed to be carved straight from the surrounding trees. Sturdy, strong, and not likely to give into the wear and tear often inflicted on furniture in a rental house.

"Have a seat." Tall and lanky motioned to the den area. "I'm Kirk Aldridge."

Terrence squinted. "The business partner."

"Yes. And friend."

"We have some questions for Mr. Parker."

"Oh. OK." A door down the hallway opened and Kirk looked in that direction.

"Hey, man. You got that hot chocolate ready? I'm…" Stuart Parker's voice trailed off as he walked into the room.

"Mr. Parker, I'm Officer Cooper." Terrence motioned to his partner. "This is Officer Patterson. We have a few questions for you."

"OK." Stuart sat. "What can I help you with?"

Either the guy was really good or wasn't involved in Julie's disappearance. "We, um…" Terrence nodded toward Kirk. "We have some questions of a rather delicate nature."

Kirk stood, but Stuart held his hand up. "I have no secrets, Officer Cooper. Kirk is my friend, and he knows about my past. You can ask whatever you need to with him here."

Terrence sat and held Stuart's gaze. Neither man wavered. "Mr. Parker, we have a few questions about your daughter."

Stuart's lips pulled tight then he sighed. "Rebecca. Did something happen? What trouble is she in now?"

"No, sir. It's not Rebecca." Back to Rebecca again. Did he even remember Julie? Or was his deflection a cover?

Stuart's eyes clouded. He leaned forward. "Emma? Something's wrong with Emma?"

"No, sir. Not Emma." How long would it take the man to get to Julie?

Stuart's brow creased. "Darlene?"

"No, sir." Terrence inspected every minute detail of the man's face. Finally, understanding lit in his eyes.

"Julia. Something's wrong with Julia."

"Yes, sir. We were wondering when you last saw Julie."

Stuart diverted his gaze to his lap. "About a month ago."

"A month ago? You know where she lives?"

Stuart nodded and met Terrence's gaze once again. "I've known for years. She's my daughter after all."

"Have you ever contacted her?"

He shook his head. "No. Frances and Julia seemed to be doing fine. They've moved on with their lives and seemed happy. My reentering it would have only caused more pain."

Kirk stood. "I'll get the hot chocolate." He strode across the room to the kitchen.

"Why don't you tell me more about knowing

where Fran and Julie live?"

Kirk returned and handed Terrence and Patterson each a half-full mug. He went back to the kitchen, grabbed the other two for him and Parker, and sat. The look on his face didn't portray curiosity. No, it was more a look of...support.

His mug cupped in both hands, Mr. Parker began. "I'm sure you know quite a bit about my background, Officer Cooper. I was not a nice person as a young man. I was angry and scared and knew only what my father had taught me. I drank and hurt the people closest to me. A lot. I'll admit that." He sipped his hot chocolate.

"In 2000, I finally hit a brick wall. I'd gotten thrown into jail for my third DUI. When I came out, I had nowhere to go. My dad had died, and my mother didn't want another angry drunk in her house. No one else wanted me either. My probation officer recommended rehab, a program called Elam House." He paused a moment, staring into his cup, then looked up again. "They took me in and taught me how to live clean. Really, they taught me how to live. To build a new life founded on God instead of on hatred. Within a few years, I started my own business, met Pauline, and began a new life."

"And Julie?"

Stuart sipped his hot chocolate then sighed. "Pauline's the one who encouraged me to look for my girls. Darlene's father had disappeared when she was an infant. Pauline thought that I should go to my girls and make amends. It's part of the twelve-step program. It wasn't too hard to find Frances and Julia. She'd used her mother's maiden name."

"But?"

A smile turned up Stuart's lips. "But I loved my daughter. I stood in the distance the day she graduated college. I watched her come out of the church the day she got married. I don't want to hurt my daughter any more than I already have. But I don't want to miss out completely on her life, either."

Terrence studied the man. Nothing shouted fabrication. He had to consider that the man could really be a reformed drunk concerned about his daughter and content to observe her life from afar, but it seemed near impossible. Most people didn't deserve that much benefit of doubt. However, nothing he was seeing or hearing was adding up to what he'd suspected.

"What about Rebecca? You thought we might be here about her. So did your wife."

Stuart's smile disappeared, and his eyes darkened. "I found Rebecca, too. She lived through more than Julia. She left when she was a teenager. Rebecca doesn't live far from my wife and me. I've tried to help her. She's not been open to my help. Yet."

"Help her how?"

"Pauline and I have offered her a place to live. But she has to get clean first. She has to give up her lifestyle. Right now, she dances at a club for a living. She's an addict. We take her food, buy her decent clothes, but she doesn't want anything from me." Resolve sharpened Stuart's features. "I won't give up, though. I found sobriety and so can she."

The information spun and swirled in Terrence's mind. He'd hoped Stuart Parker had been responsible for Julie's disappearance. The case would've been simple. He'd have been back in bed by midnight and have nothing but paperwork to take care of the next day. The clarity of the case vanished as thoroughly as had Julie Montgomery.

"Have you been here all day, Mr. Parker?"

"Yes. We stopped for breakfast on the way, checked into the cabin about seven thirty, and hit the slopes when they opened at nine."

Terrence studied his face. "You have your ski ticket? Or a receipt from breakfast?"

"Yes, to the ski ticket. I'll have to check on the restaurant bill." Stuart left the room, returning a moment later with his ski pass stamped at 9:00 AM. He also handed Terrence a crumpled receipt from a local restaurant with the current date on it and a time of a few minutes after seven. A pretty air-tight alibi.

Terrence closed his book after recording the information. "Mind if we take a look around? Check out the cabin, look at your car? Just to say we've covered all our bases?"

"Sure." Stuart stood. "I'll get the keys."

He returned a moment later, his keys jingling as they dangled from his extended hand.

"Patterson, you take the car." His partner grimaced. His seniority benefited him, allowing him to be the one to inspect the house, avoiding exposure to the frozen elements. He grinned as Patterson took the keys.

After checking every nook and cranny of the two bedroom, one bathroom cabin, Terrence cracked the front door open, braving the blast of cold air as he checked on Patterson. His head shake told Terrence they were done. He tossed the keys over and headed to the patrol car.

Terrence caught the keys, swatted the door shut, and turned to Stuart. "Thanks, Mr. Parker. We're sorry to have bothered you."

Stuart accepted the keys. "Officer Cooper. You never told me why you're here. What's happened?"

"Mr. Parker, your daughter's missing. It seems she was taken from outside her work around seven this morning."

Tears filled Stuart's eyes. He stepped back. "No. Not Julia."

"I'm sorry, Mr. Parker. With your history, we had to look into you first."

"I understand. Is there something else I can do? Can I help in any way?"

"I don't think so. You've been helpful answering our questions." Terrence slipped out the open door. A bitter wind blasted him, swirling snow around him and making him wish he'd grabbed his coat that morning.

"Please let me know if there's anything else I can do. Anything." Stuart's eyes pleaded with Terrence. The man probably would have been better off not knowing.

"I will."

He rushed to the car, slamming the door shut and the wind out.

A shivering Patterson greeted him. "Now what?"

"I have no idea."

In an Instant

SEVEN

The room grew dark as the sun set. Julie's teeth chattered, getting worse as the shadows in the room grew longer. Nausea continued in waves and her bladder alerted her to other needs. She clamped her teeth together in an attempt to keep them quiet and concerted effort not to call out for relief.

She'd wait. Better to let him cool off before asking for anything.

The bedroom door burst open and warm air rushed in. He stood behind the threshold, another bowl of steaming soup in hand. His brown eyes looked black in the faint light. The glow from the room behind him exaggerated the wild look of his unkempt hair. "Are we in a better mood yet?"

She stared at him and spoke in a low voice. "I need to use the bathroom."

"Ahh. Interesting dilemma you have." He backed out of the room only to return a moment later holding a TV tray in his free hand. He set it next to the bed and placed the bowl on it. "You need to eat and get your strength up. You look pale and weak. If you eat, you go to the bathroom."

"I really need to go. How am I supposed to ingest soup on a full bladder?" She glanced up at her hands. "Or like this?"

"Fine." He pulled the gun from the back of his waistline and gestured between her and the far wall. "You go to the bathroom and come right back. Then you eat."

He slowly untied each hand. "No funny business. No kicking. No running. I don't want to hurt you, but this gun is much faster than you."

She fought the desire to laugh. She couldn't count how many times she had heard, 'I don't want to hurt you,' only to have it followed by a collection of bruises.

"No funny business." She held her gaze and voice steady. He'd seen her a wreck and helpless once. She wouldn't let him see her that way again.

He untied one foot. "Leave the door open."

"No."

His eyebrows arched. He steadied the gun in her direction. "I make the rules. You follow them."

Scooting back in the bed, she crossed her arms. "I close the door to the bathroom or I go right here. I remember how you love body fluids and odorous smells."

He narrowed his eyes. She'd hit a nerve and would have smiled at finally getting one up on him if she wasn't shaking inside.

"Fine. But I'm timing you. You have two minutes." He untied the last rope.

She slid off the bed opposite the side he sat by. Three quick steps and she closed the bathroom door. Hoisting her layers of skirting and sitting on the toilet, she examined the tiny room. No vent. Not even a window. She washed her hands. The sink stood on a pedestal, no storage cabinet beneath. She tried the mirror. Not the kind that had a medicine storage cabinet behind it. A shower-tub combo completed her examination.

"Thirty seconds."

The bathroom held no hope. No way to signal something was wrong. Nowhere anything useful could be hidden. She sighed and opened the door.

"That's a good girl. Now come over here and eat."

She climbed onto the bed and crossed her legs. The freedom to sit up and move again energized her.

He held a spoonful of soup toward her, almost like a mother would feed an ill child. She knew better. His kindness served only to manipulate her. She wasn't that girl anymore.

"I feed myself."

He stared at her, spoon in mid-air. "You feed yourself, you have one arm tied."

She held out her left arm.

He dropped the spoon in the soup, splattering the tray. He grabbed the rope and retied it, cinching the knot tight enough to sting.

Julie scooped one spoonful and swallowed it. Her stomach rolled. Maybe it had been too long since she'd eaten. She scooped another bite then set the spoon in the bowl. "Crackers."

He jerked his gaze from the window. "What?"

"Crackers. Can I have some crackers?"

He rose from the chair without a word. His mask of kindness gone, he scowled in her direction. Moments later, he tossed a pack of saltines on the bed by her.

She'd caught him off guard but angered him. She needed to keep him calm. "I can't open it with one hand."

His eyes narrowed again.

She wiggled her left hand. "Only one hand. I can't open the crackers."

He plopped down in the chair and reached over for the package. The seal gave, and he set it back down on the bed.

The dry cracker soothed her stomach. She ate a few more bites of soup and a handful of crackers. He said nothing else.

"I'm done." She uncrossed her legs and lay down on her side. Her eyes drooped.

"But you haven't even finished the soup."

"I'm not really hungry." Sleep. She needed sleep much more than food at the moment. She was just so tired.

Her eyes popped open. He had the bowl, crackers, and tray and was heading out of the room. "What's today?"

He spun to face her. "What?"

"What's today?"

"Tuesday. Why?"

She closed her eyes, calculating. She opened them

again. "The date. What's the date?"

"Umm, the eleventh, I think. Why?" He barked the question.

"My mom's birthday is Thursday."

"That's it?"

"Well..."

"Well, what?"

"I, um, I'm going to need to go to the store."

He laughed. "The store? Do you think I'm crazy or stupid?"

She lowered her gaze. "I know you don't like anything to do with 'girly stuff.' If you don't want to have lots of stuff to deal with, then I need to go to the store tomorrow."

"You're putting me on. You're trying to trick me."

She curled her knees up closer to her chest and closed her eyes. "OK. Take the chance."

He growled. But when he left, he didn't close the door.

Pulling the sheet and blanket up to her chin with her free hand, she gave in to the overwhelming call to enter dreamland.

~*~

Julie gulped, straining to get air. Her throat was constricted and she was running, fleeing from something unknown.

She broke out of her nightmare and crept into

consciousness, chest rising and falling. Heart racing. Her eyes flew open. Darkness surrounded her. A faint glow from the other room filtered through the doorway. Her mind was clouded, foggy. Where was she?

She tried to roll on her side. A rope tugged at her wrists, but her legs moved freely. She'd woken from an imagined nightmare to a real one.

Tears pushed their way through. Oh, God, I'm trying. I don't understand. Why is this happening?

No answer came. Only the words from her prayers earlier. He was with her no matter where she was. Even abducted and tied to a bed.

Her heart slowed. She forced away the panic coursing through her veins, repeating God's words over and over. She had nothing else to cling to.

Closing her eyes against the dark and unknown, she pictured Luke. She missed him so much. How was he doing? He had to be frantic.

Tears rolled down her cheeks. She was so sorry he had to go through this.

Her longing for home, for Luke, for her mother flowed until the pillow beneath her head was soaked. She swallowed back a sob. She had to figure a way out.

But how? She didn't even know where she was. When he took her to the store, she might be able to signal someone.

She had no way to write a note. And he'd be practically glued to her side. If he carried the gun, she'd be putting others in danger if she tried to get away in public. But if she thought through it enough, she could figure something out.

Exhaustion took over and she closed her eyes. New words and phrases pushed their way through her fears. *As the deer pants for water, so my soul pants for You, God.*

Psalm 42. She'd memorized it in a Sunday school challenge last year. Snippets filled her mind. *I pour out my soul. Put your hope in God. My soul is downcast within me, so I will remember You. My soul pants for You.*

She'd memorized the words but hadn't felt them before. She had never panted for God, needed Him so desperately. Starting back at the beginning, she whispered God's words back to Him, allowing them to calm her and lull her back to sleep.

~*~

Terrence smacked his alarm and groaned. Having arrived home after midnight, he'd set the alarm for six. Usually six hours energized him. But he hadn't slept soundly and woke this morning with the knowledge of an unfinished case. An urgent, unfinished case.

He'd called Luke Montgomery after leaving the interview with Stuart Parker. Luke sounded tired and discouraged. They had all hoped the first lead would take them to Julie. It hadn't. That fact bugged Terrence throughout the night.

Rolling out of bed, he pulled on his workout clothes, brushed his teeth, and grabbed his gym bag.

He popped a couple aspirin and swiped two protein bars from the kitchen cabinet on his way out the door. A good workout would invigorate him for the day and perhaps help him in finding the missing piece in this case.

An hour later, he strode into the station looking for Manning. He'd left the third shift investigator on research duty. Leaving the case in someone else's hands stuck him like a thorn under his fingernail, but he'd have caused himself more grief working through the night. He spotted Manning leaning against Martin's desk wolfing down a sausage biscuit.

"Break time, boys?"

Manning pushed off the desk. "End of shift breakfast. You know how it is."

"Yeah. 'Cept for my shift's starting. You got anything for me?"

Manning headed toward his desk. Terrence followed. "Some, but not much. And I doubt anything useful. The girl looks as clean as you said. Of course, I didn't find anything more on the father other than what you had. He really does look clean for the last..." Manning rifled through some papers. "...ten years."

"I hoped it was him, but he has a strong alibi, and he's nothing like I expected."

The now off-duty officer yawned and leaned back in his chair. "Looked into the husband, too. Couldn't do any interviews, of course, but he's coming off as fresh as just-cut wood. Might want to have someone scrounge around and talk to some coworkers or friends today, though, just to make sure."

Terrence nodded. "Thanks. I'll get Patterson or Scruggs on it."

"I pulled the girl's social media. All tame stuff. Scripture quotes, lame video shares, cozy things shared between friends. No secret boyfriend messages or anything. Nothing stood out. She has over four hundred friends. I've made a list of the people she interacts with most." Manning handed him a stack of papers. "There's also a list of people she attended high school with, people from community college, and co-workers. The rest aren't categorized."

"OK. What else?"

"There really isn't anything else. She and her mom lived in Lynchburg where she went to public school and community college. She moved to Williamsburg a few years ago and married Luke Montgomery this year."

"What about past boyfriends?"

"Not that I saw. I put in the request for her cell phone records."

Terrence bristled. He'd wasted a whole day on a false lead. Now Julie Montgomery had been missing twenty-four hours. He needed more information. "Thanks."

He tossed the stack of papers onto his desk as he strode to the coffee pot. A hot cup of black caffeine might do what his workout and shower hadn't. He took a steaming swallow, scorching his tongue. Be more patient next time.

Dropping onto his chair, he stared at the disarray on his desk. He couldn't figure out why this case bothered him so much. He usually dealt with druggies, thieves, and wife abusers. Rarely did a case come along that wasn't cut and dry. The occasional robbery took a little longer to figure out, but the evidence almost always added up. Never had he had a case thrown in his lap with such a lack of evidence. No trail of clues leading to a logical and easily-proven conclusion.

He worked his jaw. He preferred working alone. Partners were a necessity on the force, but he resisted one at every turn. The fact that he'd relied so much on Patterson the last couple of days irked him. He'd made himself the man he was, choosing to work hard in school and do what it took to get in and excel at the academy.

His friends had given him plenty of grief, but Terrence had always wanted to be a cop. And he'd done everything required to become one. He didn't need any help obtaining success, nor did he need any help doing his job.

His coffee ceased steaming, and he risked another sip. This time the black liquid warmed him instead of scorching his tongue.

He read through the lists, trying to determine where to start. Finding the right person to interview who might have the right information would be like trying to find a wheat penny in a five-gallon bucket of copper coins. Julie didn't have time for him to sift through hundreds of friends.

Start at the beginning. Classic investigation rule. He needed to go back to where Julie was taken. Interview more people. See if anyone saw anything. He groaned. Even doing those interviews would take him most of the day.

He looked across the room. Patterson sat at his desk. He picked up the phone instead of hollering.

He answered on the first ring. "Patterson."

"What you got going on today?" Terrence met his gaze and a smile formed.

"I wondered how long it would take you to ask for help."

"This long. We need to go back to Colonial Williamsburg. Someone else could have seen something and didn't realize what they saw."

"Sounds good. When do you want to leave?"

He stood. "Twenty minutes ago."

Patterson nodded, hung up the phone, and grabbed his gear.

Hanging up his own phone, Terrence grabbed the stack of papers Manning had given him. The phone rang as he pulled his car keys out of his pocket.

"Cooper."

"Officer Cooper, it's Luke Montgomery."

"Mr. Montgomery. I don't have any more information. I'm heading out right now. I'm on your wife's case. It's top priority."

A sigh filtered over the line. "I tried to go to work this morning, but after smashing two fingers in five minutes, I decided work isn't the best distraction. I want to do something to help."

"I don't think…" He eyed the stack of papers. Luke would be the best person to go through her friend list. He and Ms. Fran. "You know, there is something you can do. We pulled Julie's friend list off her social media. They're organized by affiliation. Do you think you can go through them and mark the people she's closest to?"

"Yeah, I could do that."

"You could also get Ms. Fran to help you. She'd know Julie's friends from high school and college."

"OK." Hope permeated his voice.

"It's important to go through these lists, but they may not give us what we need. It's just part of the procedure. We can hope that something helpful comes up, but we also need to stay realistic that it could only lead to more interviews and dead ends."

"That's OK. At least I'll be doing something."

"All right, then. I'll drop the lists off at Ms. Fran's house in about a half hour."

He replaced the receiver and met Patterson's stare. "What?"

He crossed his arms and grinned. "You like these people."

"I'm working a case."

Patterson grinned. "A case for people you're beginning to like."

"I'm working. Are you going to do likewise or stand here grinning like a hyena all day?" He headed out, half wishing Patterson wouldn't follow him. Moments later, though, the passenger door of his squad car closed with Patterson sitting shotgun.

EIGHT

Terrence led Patterson from the parking lot to Julie's workplace. He walked through the doorway, and the scent of cinnamon tickled his nose. Sue met his gaze and raised her eyebrows, hope written on her face. He shook his head, and her face fell. The girl working with her caught his eye. Her pitch-black hair was pulled back and peeked out from an eighteenth century cap. She wore the same style of dress as Sue but in brilliant blue instead of pale yellow. Her soft brown eyes met his gaze and she grinned. His heart rate doubled.

What a smile.

"Nothing?" Sue's voice stole his attention from the dark, warm eyes. Her hands rested on her rounded stomach.

"No, I'm sorry, not yet." He glanced back at the girl in blue.

"I'm sorry. This is Maggie. She's filling in for Julie."

He stuck out his hand. "Nice to meet you. Sorry

it's under these circumstances." Her hand was small and warm in his. Freckles dotted her hand and arm.

"It's a pleasure to meet you, too. And, yes, I wish it was for a different reason."

Pulling his gaze and hand away from Maggie's, he looked at Sue. "We've come up empty with our first lead. Patterson here" —he tilted his head—"is helping me out with questioning. We want to talk to everyone who would have been coming to work the same time as Julie and might have seen something."

Sue's eyes widened and she raised her eyebrows. "Everyone?"

He grinned. "As many as possible. Those who would've crossed her path." His grin faded. "We'll need a list."

"I can help you with some. The best person to talk to is Margaret in human resources. She'd have the full list of employees and where they work."

"OK. Thanks." He recorded Margaret's name and the location of human resources in his notebook. "Have you thought of anything else that might help?"

Tears pooled in Sue's eyes. "No. I keep wracking my brain. I didn't see anything and can't think of anything Julie ever said that might be a clue."

"That's OK. I didn't expect there'd be anything new." Turning to Maggie, he met her gaze, pausing a moment before asking the question. "Were you working yesterday morning?"

"I didn't get to work until ten." She fluttered her eyelashes.

"OK. Thanks."

He turned and followed Patterson out. "I think we should start with the workers in the vicinity. Then we can go see Margaret in HR."

Patterson eyed the area. "Sounds good. You have the pictures of Mrs. Montgomery in case someone doesn't know her by name?"

Pulling the printed pictures from the back of his notebook, Terrence handed him two of each. "Here. I'll head east, and you go west." He checked his watch. "We'll meet at Colonel's Tavern at noon."

"All right."

He headed toward the next building to the left. Ten minutes later he trudged back out with no more information than he had before. The next three buildings resulted with the same lack of new information and a steady increase in his frustration. Everyone knew Julie, but no one had seen her yesterday morning. This woman, whose family loved and adored her, also held the respect of her coworkers and acquaintances. The darkening clouds overhead matched his mood. Time ticked away and Julie's life became more and more endangered. And all he could do was spin his wheels.

All they needed was one person who'd seen something. Just one.

Ignoring the bitter wind that blew the dark clouds in, he headed to the next buildings, asking the same questions again and again. Do you know Julie Montgomery? Did you see her yesterday morning? Have you ever seen anyone hanging around where she works? Had anyone been hanging out on the streets yesterday, looking like they didn't belong?

The answers to each question repeated themselves as frequently as he asked them. Finally, after almost two hours of questioning and turning up nothing, he stomped out into the frigid air that now contained a persistent drizzle. The cold he didn't mind. Cold plus wet he despised. He growled as he walked to the tavern where he and Patterson agreed to meet.

Walking into the dimly lit room, he spotted his current partner at a corner table, facing the entrance. Only a handful of other tables had patrons, creating a low hum of conversations. He dropped into the chair to the side instead of opposite Patterson so he could also see the door. He hung his damp coat on the back of the chair.

Patterson tapped his spoon on his mug and set it on the table. "I take it you haven't found anything useful."

He held his groan silent. He wasn't only frustrated at the lack of evidence but also that he'd become so readable. "Not a thing."

Patterson sighed and sipped a cup of coffee. "Me neither."

He eyed the young girl heading toward their table, aiming a big grin at him. "Afternoon. Can I get ya somethin' ta drink?"

"Coffee."

"OK," she drawled out in a thicker southern accent than normal for the area. "Y'all ready ta order?"

Terrence picked up his menu. "Not yet."

She bounded off, her short blond ponytail

swinging behind her. He set the menu down and turned to Patterson. "Everybody knows Julie. No one saw her yesterday."

"Same here. The rumor mill has spread pretty effectively that she's missing, but there's not even one theory as to what happened. I've never seen anything like it. There's always speculation about what happened. People love to give their opinions."

Terrence shivered. His cup of warm coffee was taking more time than it should. "It's the most aggravating case I've ever worked. How can a woman disappear and no one see anything? I'm not sure it's worth going to human resources for more names. Besides, Ms. Fran and Luke should've gotten through the friends list by now."

Patterson nodded. "I agree. I don't think we're going to find out anything else here."

The young girl with the floppy ponytail and thick accent came toward their table with Terrence's cup of coffee. Finally.

She set it down. "Y'all ready ta order yet?"

Patterson answered. "We haven't even had a chance to look at the menu."

The waitress grinned. "I'll give ya a few more minutes. What are a couple of cops doing hanging out in Colonial Williamsburg for lunch, anyhow?"

Terrence sipped his coffee, trying to get rid of his chill and let Patterson answer.

"We're investigating a disappearance."

A hand went to the waitress's hip and her eyes widened. "A disappearance?"

"A young woman left for work yesterday, parked in the employee lot, but never made it to her building."

The waitress pursed her lips. "You know, I thank I remember hearing sumthin' 'bout that yesterday."

Patterson raised his eyebrows at Terrence, who answered the unspoken question with shrugged shoulders. "Did you know Julie?"

"Julie?"

Guess that meant she didn't.

"The missing woman." Terrence answered.

"Oh. No. I just started working here this week. It's been a little crazy. I have ta get here at the crack of dawn for training then stay for lunch shift. Next week, I start on dinna shift."

Terrence leaned forward. "How early is the crack of dawn?"

The waitress rolled her eyes. "I havta be here at seven. All my friends are barely asleep when I gotta get up and get ready for work."

"And yesterday, you got here at seven?"

She grinned. "Five of."

Terrence pulled a picture out of his notebook. "This is Julie, the woman who disappeared. She was coming to work about that same time. Did you happen to see her?"

Staring at the picture, the waitress pursed her lips again. Then her mouth fell open. "You know, I think I might've."

He met Patterson's gaze. They may have just stumbled onto their first useful clue. "Where?"

She looked at him. "Passing by the candy shop,

heading toward one of the visitor parking lots. There was some guy walking with her. If it was her."

Terrence tapped the picture. "Look at the picture again. Is that the woman you saw?"

The young waitress examined the picture in her hand. Her head nodded slowly. "Yes. That's her. I remember thanking she must be walking a boyfriend or sumthin' back ta his car. But I couldn't figure out why he'd come out to see her so early in the mornin'."

Blood raced through Terrence's veins. The quickened pulse wasn't the caffeine, because he'd barely touched his coffee. Not only had this girl seen Julie, she'd seen a guy with her. "Did you get a good look at the guy?"

She dropped her hand from her hip and realization spread across her face. "You mean he might have sumthin' ta do with her disappearing? That I saw this woman with the guy who took 'er?" Her hands shook.

Terrence kept his voice calm and gaze steady. "I don't know. That's what we're trying to find out. If you did see Mrs. Montgomery with someone yesterday, you are the only one who saw her. That means you're the only person who can help us find her right now."

"I...I..." She worried her apron with both hands.

Patterson spoke up. "What's your name?"

"Chloe."

"Chloe, you're not in trouble, and there's no way you could've known something was wrong. You said yourself, you didn't know Julie. You'd never seen her before."

She continued to fidget with her apron.

"We'll need you to get with a sketch artist," Patterson continued. "What time do you get off?"

"Three."

Terrence played with his cooled off coffee cup. Three. They couldn't wait that long. They had to get moving immediately. "Is there any way you could get off early?"

"It's my third day on the job." She glanced over her shoulder.

Patterson leaned toward her and grinned. "I understand. Your job's important to you. We don't want to jeopardize it. Where's your manager? We'll explain what's going on."

"He's in back."

"OK. You run and get him, and we'll take care of the rest." Patterson assured her.

Chloe nodded, turned on her heel, and rushed off.

"Unbelievable."

Patterson sat back in his chair. "Yeah. Who'd have thought lunch would have brought us our first break?"

Impatience pumped through Terrence with every heartbeat. Hurry. Julie doesn't have time. "And when we catch our first break it's through a girl scared of her own shadow."

"Give her a break. She's young, and she just found out she's a witness to an abduction."

"Our only witness." He drummed his fingers on the table.

"I know, but we'll get more out of Chloe if we don't spook her."

"Yeah, but--" Terrence eyed the short balding man leading Chloe back to the table. She looked even younger, if that were possible.

"Hi, I'm Doug Abbott. Can I help you gentlemen?"

Patterson held his badge out in his left hand and stuck out his right. "Patterson. This is my partner, Cooper."

Terrence shook the man's hand.

"We're looking into the disappearance of Julie Montgomery."

"I heard something about that. She works here at CW and never made it in yesterday."

"Right. We've been questioning employees all morning and turns out Chloe here"—Patterson nodded at her—"is the only one who saw Mrs. Montgomery before she disappeared. Chloe also saw a man with Mrs. Montgomery. We need her to come to the station and meet with our sketch artist. We understand she doesn't get off until three and doesn't want to risk her job, but time's essential in a missing person case."

"Of course." The bald manager glanced back at the trembling girl. "We'll get Kasey and Rebecca to cover your tables." He turned back to Patterson. "Anything we can do to help."

"Thanks." Patterson looked at Terrence. "Guess we'll get lunch later." He threw a few dollar bills on the table. "Chloe, do you know where the station is?"

She shook her head.

"All right. We'll take you to your car. Then you can follow us to the station."

"OK."

Back in the car and in control again, Terrence had to admit to himself, Patterson was good. Where he would have shot off questions like a machine gun, Patterson tossed them out like he was playing corn hole. He evaluated his target, took careful aim, and pitched the question gently. But he always hit the mark.

He checked the rearview mirror. Chloe's little silver car still followed them. Soon they'd have a picture of the guy responsible for Julie's disappearance.

NINE

Luke shoved the papers across his mother-in-law's dining room table. An anguished moan escaped. "How can I know so little about my wife? I don't even know half her online friends."

Fran put a hand on his arm. "Julie's a private person. You know that. She holds things close."

"Yes," he said through gritted teeth. "But I'm her husband. She shouldn't have kept things from me. I'd have understood. I'd still love her."

"I'm sure she didn't see it as hiding things from you, Luke. It's just who she is. Julie observes; she takes it all in, but she doesn't let much out. She shares only what's necessary."

He pushed the chair from the table and stood. "But I love her. I thought I knew her inside out."

He paced in the small space between the table and the kitchen counter. "Why didn't she trust me? She couldn't even tell me about her father." He stopped pacing and turned towards Fran. "How could she not tell me her father abused her?"

Compassion filled his mother-in-law's eyes. "Luke, this is about Julie, not you. She never talked about her father after we left."

"Never?"

"Not a single word."

He deflated and dropped into a chair. "How could she keep that in?"

"I don't know. When we lived at the shelter, we had counseling sessions galore. Family counseling, group counseling, individual counseling. She talked about school, what toys she liked, and what she wanted to be when she grew up, but she refused to talk about her father."

Shaking his head, Luke looked at his mother-in-law in disbelief. "That's crazy. She couldn't get past it if she bottled it up."

"Don't you think I know that?" Her voice cracked along with her composure. "What could I do? I couldn't force her to talk. We tried everything. Play therapy. Exposing her to other victims' stories. Asking direct questions, asking subtle questions. She ignored all attempts we made. Even though she didn't talk about it, she seemed to be OK. Her obsession with organization and order may have been peculiar for a child her age, but overall, she appeared unaffected." Her voice grew higher as she spoke.

Luke sighed. "She's always been in such control. Everything perfect."

"Because the first eight years of her life were chaotic, and she had no control over anything."

"I should have known."

Fran's hands covered his. "You couldn't have known. Julie doesn't let anyone get a glimpse of the trauma she's been through."

He stared at the framed picture hanging on the wall behind Fran. Julie at about ten years old, sitting on a swing with her feet planted firmly on the ground. The sadness in her eyes had escaped his notice before. He'd always focused on her smile. A smile that lit up everyone she aimed it at.

Returning his gaze to Fran, Luke reached out and held her hands. "And now this. Julie must be scared to death."

"We don't know what she's facing, but I do know she's strong. Julie's a survivor. She'll get through. And you'll have a chance to talk to her about everything."

"I hope so." He looked at the stack of papers they had been going through. "I guess the best thing we can do now is get this list whittled down for Officer Cooper."

"That and pray." Tears filled her eyes.

"Right." He lifted the top sheet. "I've highlighted our closest friends and a couple coworkers. But we've talked to Sue, Heather, and Dawn. If anyone would know about something going on with Julie, they would. Or so I'd have thought."

Leaning over, Fran inhaled deeply and squinted at the papers. "OK. We'll give their names and numbers to Terrence. He may want to contact them himself."

"And I'm sure he's questioned her coworkers. But I marked them, too."

Fran ran her finger down the list of names again,

nodding.

He picked up the next sheet. "What about the college list?"

"I've highlighted the names of the three girls I remember Julie talking about most."

Glancing over the list, Luke nodded. "I recognize these names, too. No one else stands out."

Fran handed him the third list. "I marked two names on this list, volleyball teammates from high school. They were the only girls Julie ever brought to the house."

"And the last list?"

"A few names I recognize from church, umm, a few from your family and that's it."

He skimmed the final list. "Yeah. That's about it."

He shoved the papers aside and covered his face with his hands.

Where was she? And why had she kept so much from him?

Heat rushed to his face. He stood with his fist clenched, kicking the chair back out of his way. He grabbed the papers, rattling them in his fist as he shook them. "This. This is all I have of my wife. A list of names. She's disappeared like a mirage. An apparition." Luke flung the papers across the room. "That's all she let me see. A phantom." His tone was loud and harsh.

He ignored Fran's wide eyes and stormed out of the house. A cold wind blasted him. Had he not been fueled by the intense burning inside, he'd have gone back for his coat. Instead, he pulled out his phone. A picture of Julie greeted him and a groan like a wounded animal escaped from him.

His Julie. Gone. Hurt. Dealing with who knew what else all on her own. Again.

He resisted the urge to run. Instead, he slipped into the driver's seat of his truck and clicked his way to Mark's number. His friend answered after three rings.

"Hello?"

"Hey. It's me. That boxing ring still available?"

"Yeah, man. Anytime."

Luke cranked the engine. "Now?"

Mark's voice lowered. "Yeah. You want to talk first?"

"No."

"OK. I'll send your name to the gate."

He copied the directions to the base fitness center and flew out of the driveway.

~*~

Fran rushed to the living room window. Luke's truck sped down the road. Tears bubbled to the surface and overflowed like a forgotten pot of water. Her hands shook.

"Oh, God. How can I take this? My Julie. And now Luke. He had enough on him without all this."

She closed her eyes. The memory of angry, bloodshot eyes shooting threats at her and the girls flooded her mind. Hard hands hitting, squeezing, throwing. She could almost smell stale beer and angry sweat. Two nights before she and Julie left were the worst. Fran hadn't reacted as she always had. No crying or begging. Her lack of reaction poured lighter fluid on his already simmering charcoal attitude. She'd walked away thirty-six hours later with two broken ribs.

She'd been crazy to have thought it would get better. Too many times she had hoped Stuart really meant it when he said he was sorry. Bile rose in her throat as the memories assaulted her. She never should have stayed as long as she had.

Fran inhaled fresh, fragrant air. She took in the smell of a pecan pie candle. She breathed out ugly memories and pain. Three more deep breaths calmed the shaking.

Opening her eyes, she let her gaze take in the details of her home. The pictures on the wall showed happy faces. The window blinds were raised to let light in. No threat infiltrated her house. The danger had been eliminated years before.

So, why the threat to Julie now?

Giving into the weight of the facts that threatened her, she fell to her knees. "God, I can't do this. I can't sit here unable to help my baby girl. Not knowing where she is, if she's OK, what's happening to her, is killing me." Tears flowed. "I can't be strong for Luke. I don't understand either. Was there something I missed? Is her disappearance my fault?"

Question after question rose from her lips. They flew instantaneously to the Lord she believed in and had worshipped for more than a decade.

"I thought You wouldn't give us more than we can handle. I can't handle this." Her voice rose. "Why have You let this happen?"

Throat raw and heart drowning, she dropped to the floor in a heap and soaked the carpet with her tears. Time ticked away as wordless groans reached out to God.

After what felt like hours, she stretched out across on the floor.

Fran's mind trailed back to a Bible study she'd gone through the year before. The author talked about breathing in carpet fibers while praying. Now she had that personal experience. She'd poured out her heart in tears and prayer and had nothing left. She'd desperately sought an answer. For her. For Julie. For Luke.

Her cheek rested on the Berber. Her eyes drooped. Words pushed through her drowsiness.

My grace is sufficient for you, for My power is made perfect in weakness.

The words penetrated the stillness. No. They came from the stillness.

My grace is sufficient for you, for My power is made perfect in weakness.

She edged her way to a sitting position. This was not the answer she'd been looking for. She wanted a clue. A hint at something they'd missed. Something that would lead them to Julie.

Words surrounded her heart and rolled through her mind. Weakness. Fran had felt weak before.

Helpless. She never expected to feel it again. Especially now that she knew God.

She had come to despise weakness. She'd had to be strong to leave Stuart. To start a new life for herself and Julie. She'd been strong for Julie's friends who had come to her for advice, for her own friends through difficulties. She had prided herself in her strength, even in her faith. This she couldn't bear. The possible loss of her daughter was beyond her strength to handle.

The words God said to her highlighted her weakness, but not in the berating, critical way she viewed weakness.

"You want me to be weak, God?"

Trust in the Lord with all your heart and lean not on your own understanding.

Realization shot through her. She hadn't been trusting God. Not really. She'd become strong. Independent. Self-reliant. *Just like Julie.*

As long as Fran could rely on herself, stay strong and bear anything that came her way, she didn't have to trust God. Not really. Not with the details.

Weakness. Strength.

Trust. Understanding.

Words of exchange. She could not handle this. Julie had disappeared, and Fran's life had changed in an instant. She'd been able to hold things together as long as she had to be strong for Luke. For their friends. But as Luke cracked, and the hours stretched, hopelessness filled her.

"OK, God. I can't do this. It's too much for me to

bear. But it's not too much for You. I give You my weakness for Your strength. I give You my understanding and choose to trust You completely. Let Julie do the same. Draw her close to You, Lord. I know she's in Your hands. Keep her safe and *please* bring her back to me."

TEN

Julie grabbed the bathroom sink and steadied herself. Nausea washed over her again and again. She closed her eyes and held on, waiting for it to pass. It didn't. She barely made it over the toilet in time.

Sweat beaded her forehead. She wiped her face and mouth with toilet paper. At the sink again, she washed the bile out of her mouth. A couple handfuls of water refreshed her, and she returned to changing clothes.

He had thrown a sweatshirt and pair of jeans in her room, declaring, "Change clothes. We're going to the store."

At least he'd been angry enough to leave her alone. He couldn't blame her, though. Monthly cycles were out of her control.

Pulling the dress and layers of underclothes off, she washed herself with the hand soap and sink water. He'd given her only five minutes to change. That didn't leave time for a real shower. The jeans and sweatshirt were much more comfortable. Lighter and less restrictive than her work costume. She was freer to move about unencumbered by all the extra layers.

Freedom to move. The real freedom she desired was to escape from his grasp. To get far enough away so he couldn't touch her again. Ever.

Would today be her chance? She'd convinced him to take her away from the house. Into town even. Whatever town that might be. She could study the landscape and possibly figure out where she was. Check out all the routes and buildings close by.

She opened the door. He stood in the frame leading to the room she hadn't seen yet.

"Ready?"

"I just need to get my shoes on."

"Get them, then," he growled.

She did so and walked slowly toward him. "I'm ready."

He lifted the gun in his left hand and aimed it at her chest. "This will be with me at all times. Don't forget it." He slid the pistol into the back of his waistband then pulled a tan cloth from his pocket, stretching it out before her eyes and smiled.

"And you, my dear, will be wearing this. At least for now." Taking a step forward, he covered Julie's eyes with the cloth and tied it behind her head. A moment later, he slipped a pair of glasses on top of the cloth, the earpieces hooking over her ears.

Her throat tightened. How in the world would she be able to tell anything? She couldn't see. Couldn't plan.

Oh, God. Help me!

He tugged on her arm. "Let's go. Your chariot awaits."

Bile rose in her throat again. She'd love to vomit all over him but concentrated on keeping it down. No telling what he'd do if she pushed him over the edge. He'd left bruises on her for much less. She breathed in and out slowly and deeply until the nausea passed.

He shoved her into a car seat and both doors clicked shut, first hers, then his. The engine cranked, and the car began to roll. Popping and crunching reached her ears.

Gravel. The driveway was gravel. She couldn't see, but she could still feel and listen. The car edged along, swerving left and right, often, as if trying to miss potholes common to gravel driveways. She began to count. *One thousand. Two thousand. Three thousand.* In just over a minute, the car stopped, turned left and sailed. *Pavement.*

"You've never been so quiet." He interrupted her counting.

"You've never been so desperate."

The car sped up. "I'm not desperate. I'm taking what's mine."

Every ounce of her body wanted to scream, "I'm not yours!" But that would set him off. She knew not to argue with a mad man—especially a violent one. She remained silent.

Julie had no idea how fast the car was going, so counting would do her no good. *I can't do a thing. Not one single thing to help myself get out of this mess. And if I can't help myself, where will help come from? How in the world will they be able to find me?*

Opening her eyes, nothing but faint light filtered through the blindfold and what she assumed were large, dark sunglasses. She closed her eyes again.

A song floated through her mind. At first, the tune came softly, the lyrics unintelligible. Then they became clear. They matched the verse that had come to mind moments earlier.

I lift my eyes up to the hills. Where does my help come from? My help comes from the Lord, the maker of heaven and earth.

Her eyes flew open. Nothing. Road noise was the only sound. No radio played. Certainly, if there had been one on, it wouldn't have been a station playing those words. She closed her eyes, willing the music back. The words. They had been the answer to her plea. They rolled through her mind.

Where does my help come from? My help comes from the Lord, the maker of heaven and earth.

God was in control. He knew where she was, and she had to hang on to that. She could focus on the desperateness of her situation or continue to praise God in the midst of this storm. If she escaped, she'd worship Him. If she had to return to that cabin with him, she would raise her tied hands in praise.

No matter what, God had not, and would not, leave her.

Tears filled her eyes. Hadn't she been through this already in the last day and a half? She'd determined to trust God but couldn't see Him working. Her inability to sense God or her surroundings, not knowing, made her feel so out of control. Helpless and hopeless.

She'd placed her faith in God years ago. Now she needed to dig deeper into her faith than she'd ever had to before to trust Him through this. Praise Him in this.

The cloth caressing her eyes soaked in the couple of escaped tears.

Julie had asked for help, and God sent her a song. A song about praising Him in a storm. About lifting her eyes to Him for help. She couldn't see Him. She'd seen enough of Him in her life, though.

OK, God. I give it to You. I might try to pick it back up in a few minutes, but don't let me forget, You are a mighty, holy, and loving God no matter where I am.

The car slowed and turned right. She counted a handful of seconds as it crept, turned left, then came to a stop.

He slipped the blindfold out beneath the glasses, holding the dark shades securely against her face. "Leave them on."

She straightened the glasses, refusing to meet his eyes.

"We'll be here five minutes. No longer. I'll always be within eyesight and have this."

She peeked at him as he shifted his coat to reveal the gun. He then dug in his pocket and handed her several crumpled bills. "Get what you need, pay for it, and we're out of here. Do not take the sunglasses off. Do not try to signal anyone. No funny business. If I can't have you, no one will. And if you try anything stupid, you'll be taking a few innocent people out with you."

Julie bit her bottom lip and nodded. The shaking in her hands returned. He walked around the car and opened her door. She stepped out and shoved her hands in her front pockets. She didn't have to let him see her shaking.

They were at a convenience store. One she'd never seen before. She had no idea where he'd taken her.

He stayed glued to her side as they walked up the sidewalk and through the double glass doors. Spotting the aisle she needed, Julie headed toward it, ignoring his presence as best she could. He stopped at the end of the aisle pretending to browse Christmas trinkets.

Stopping in front of the feminine products, she glanced over her shoulder. He met her gaze. She refocused on the items in front of her, pretending to decide on the right brand. She plucked one package up and cut her eyes to the left. He wasn't watching. She snatched up two more packages. The item she said she needed and what she *really* needed. Tucking the smaller box between the two bulkier packages, she turned to leave the aisle. He shifted to a display directly across from the checkout counter as she waited for the customer in front of her to finish his purchase.

Her gaze gravitated to the items waiting to be scanned for the customer ahead of her. A slight smile settled on her lips. Kids toothbrushes, coloring books, markers, crayons, toy figurines and tiny Coke glasses. Stocking fillers, she guessed. Hopefully she, too, would one day be back to her normal life and even be able to buy her own children gobs of fun little things for Christmas.

Her smile faded as her captor caught her eye. She held her items tightly against her chest.

The man in front of her finished his transaction and grabbed up his bags. Julie turned her back to her captor to block his view of her purchases and laid them on the counter.

"Good morning." The middle-aged woman behind the register greeted her. "Did you find everything OK?"

Her voice came out in a whisper. "Yes. I–"

Behind her, *he* cleared his throat loudly. Her heart took off like a revved car engine. "Yes, ma'am."

A minute later, she held her purchases wrapped tightly in a bag next to her stomach. She exited the store, and he stepped up behind her. Silently, she got in the car, clutching the bag and its contents.

"Good girl." He leered at her. "I thought you might have had something stupid working in that little pretty mind of yours. Maybe this will work out after all."

The arrogance in his eyes turned her stomach. She laid her head on the window as another one of the now-too-consistent waves overtook her.

"Tired, my dear? You shouldn't be. You've barely gotten out of bed for two days." His laugh surrounded her like thick smoke. "Why don't you lay your seat back and rest on the way home?"

Home? Home with him increased her urge to throw up. Holding her breath, she prayed the contents left in her stomach stayed there.

"Go ahead. Lay back." The words came as a

command.

Unable to muster any strength to fight, she obeyed.

"We still need this, though." He replaced the blindfold and readjusted the sunglasses.

Julie gave into the weariness. No use trying to track their path. God had been clear that He was with her. She simply had to trust Him to get her through this and hopefully out of it. Besides, she was suddenly too tired to do anything else.

ELEVEN

Luke wiped the sweat off his face with a white rag and gulped the remaining water out of the bottle Mark had given him.

"Feel better, man?"

"Yeah."

Wiping his own sweat, Mark leaned back against the wall. "Now you wanna talk?"

Luke tossed the empty water bottle into the recycle bin ten feet away. The bottle bounced twice then plunked into the hole. "I don't know. None of this makes sense."

"No, it doesn't. I'd go crazy if Sue disappeared into thin air while on her way to work one morning. Especially with the baby on the way." Mark pushed away from the wall and shook his head. He clasped Luke's shoulder. "I have no idea what you're going through. But God does."

"That's part of what I don't understand." Luke shook his head. "Why would God let this happen? Where was He when someone snatched Julie off the street? If God loves us, why?"

Pain flickered in Mark's eyes. He blinked. "Those are answers we may never have. Not in this life, anyway. But trust me, God is still in control. He was with Julie when she disappeared, and He's with her now. He's with you, too." His voice exuded calm.

"I know that. In my head." Luke tapped his chest. "But my heart's having a hard time with it. I just want Julie back home." He didn't like the waver in his own voice but had no control left.

Mark closed his eyes. Opening his eyes, he met Luke's gaze. "We want to understand, but we're not guaranteed to understand. God asks us to trust Him. Seek Him. Obey Him."

Turning away, Mark paced back and forth. He stopped and spun to face Luke again, with compassion softening his military-hardened face. "Pour out your heart to God. Rant, rave, and scream. He can take it. But then ask Him for what you want and praise Him for providing an answer."

Luke spoke through gritted teeth. "He hasn't provided an answer."

"Yet. He will. And you can praise Him even before it comes. God is working, has already worked in this situation, even if we can't see it."

Mark was right, and he hated it. He despised the whole situation. But there was nothing else he could do. "I'll work on it. That's all I can offer."

"Good." Mark squeezed his shoulder. "But for now, why don't you work on getting a shower. You stink."

Luke sniffed. "Yeah, well, so do you."

In his truck on the way back to Fran's, he mulled over Mark's words and tried to come up with his own. His mother-in-law deserved an apology. None of this was her fault. His wife's history wasn't hers to share. Julie should've told him herself.

They would discuss it one day, but for now, he wanted to do anything possible to help find his wife and comfort Fran until they did. She always supported him and Julie and their friends, and they leaned on her during tough times. Now she needed someone to lean on. He couldn't lose it with her again.

He knocked and opened the door without waiting for an answer. The intermingled aromas of cinnamon, chocolate, and sugar invited him in. An apron-clad Fran appeared in the doorway to the kitchen.

He forced a smile. "You've been busy."

She wiped her hands on the black apron adorned with a bright green Christmas tree. "Yes. It's still almost Christmas, and I can't just sit around. I'm sure more people will come by. Might as well have something for them to nibble on."

"Smells great. And I'm famished."

Fran's lips turned up in a sad grin. "Well, come on, and I'll get you something to eat."

Luke followed her. He so wished his mother could be like this. Caring, giving, understanding. He'd ignored at least half a dozen calls from her since talking to her the day before. He didn't even care if she wanted to apologize. That, too, he'd deal with after they found Julie.

Plucking a warm chocolate chip cookie off the cooling rack, he eyed the sugar cookies cooling on wax paper. "Fran…"

She shook her head. "There's nothing to say."

He finished off his second cookie and licked the gooey chocolate off his fingers. No words came. They seemed to all get caught in his throat.

She slid the last cookies off the hot pan. "Don't spoil your appetite. How about lunch first? Soup and a grilled cheese?"

"Made from your mom's chicken soup recipe?"

"The very one and same."

"Then yes, definitely."

Fran opened the freezer and pulled out two pint containers. Luke popped a third cookie in his mouth while Fran's back was turned. She pulled out a pot and dumped in the frozen clumps of stew. This was as much home as his. For a moment, he could pretend his wife was upstairs or hadn't gotten off work yet. Everything was fine, and she'd walk through the door or call any minute.

The timer buzzed and the phone rang as Fran pulled another tray of cookies from the oven. His heart skipped a beat and he reached for the phone. "Hello?"

"This is Officer Cooper."

Not Julie. He'd probably been crazy to even think it could have been her. "Hi, Officer. This is Luke Montgomery. Have you found anything?"

"I wanted to come by and check those lists I dropped off this morning. Have you and Ms. Fran had a chance to go over them?"

Luke's hopes dashed. He wasn't calling to give them information. The stack of papers sat straightened and neat on the dinner table. "Yes, we did."

"Good. We also have a sketch we want you to look at."

"A sketch?" They had found something.

"Yes. We went back to Colonial Williamsburg today for more interviews. We came across a new waitress that thinks she saw Julie yesterday morning with a man. She's met with our sketch artist, and we want you to look at it."

A man. Someone saw Julie with a man. But if it wasn't her father, who else could it be? "OK. We'll be here."

He hung up the phone and met Fran's gaze, her eyebrows upraised. She stood by the stove stirring the now-thawing soup, her hand moving the wooden spoon in slow circles.

"Someone saw Julie."

The wooden spoon stilled. "Where?"

"He didn't say exactly but somewhere at CW yesterday morning, with a man. They have a sketch."

She rested a hand on her chest, closed her eyes. "Thank you," barely exited her lips. In a normal tone, she said, "Oh good. Maybe this is almost over. If either of us recognizes him."

"If."

Both hope and doubt rose and filled the room, battling with the rising smell of chicken vegetable soup. Despite the three-cookie appetizer he'd gobbled, his stomach growled. Boxing had taken more out of him than running usually did. He'd probably feel all the different muscles he'd used tomorrow. *Good.* Something other than his heart could hurt.

He pulled out a chair and sat at the table, reviewing the brief phone call. A sketch. This could be the clue they'd been hoping for.

What if neither of them recognized the guy?

What would happen then? The clock on the microwave glared and mocked him. Julie had been missing for thirty hours. They were well past the most important time in a missing person search. At least, that was what he'd always heard.

The picture could mean nothing. Or it could mean everything.

A plate holding a crisp, golden-brown grilled cheese and a steaming bowl of soup placed in front of him pulled Luke from his thoughts. "Thanks. This looks delicious."

"There's plenty of soup. Let me know if you want more."

"Aren't you going to have some?"

"I'm not hungry." She slid fresh cookies onto the cooling rack. "Besides, there are at least two more batches of cookies waiting to be baked. Then the sugar cookies to decorate."

The first spoonful of soup satisfied his taste buds and warmed him through. "OK, but you need to eat something."

Fran scooped raw cookie dough onto the cooled-off cookie sheet. "I will."

He ate his sandwich and two bowls of soup in

silence as Fran kept busy. He suspected they both had the same concern. Soon they'd know more about Julie's disappearance or have their hopes dashed with another dead end.

~*~

Terrence parked on the curb by Ms. Fran's house. He should've warned them. The sketch hadn't turned out to be the big lead he'd hoped for. The guy was smart. He wore a hat, sunglasses, and had a beard. Also, Chloe had only seen his profile.

He opened the file and looked at the sketch again. If anyone could recognize the guy, it'd be a miracle. No hair color. No eyes. No jaw line. All they had was a nose profile and a cheekbone. He hoped it'd be enough to trigger something in Mr. Montgomery or Ms. Fran's memory. For all their sakes, especially Julie's.

Movement at the front door grabbed his attention. Ms. Fran stood waiting. He strode up the driveway and offered her a tight smile as he drew close. She held the door open. The smells of Christmas pulled him through the door. "I've just finished some cookies. And there's a pot of soup on the stove. Are you hungry, Terrence?"

Just like his mom. Focusing on food to avoid her true concerns. "No. I grabbed something on the way over. But thank you."

"Well, you let me know if you change your mind."

She guided him into the kitchen.

He didn't sit. He met their expectant faces. "It may be nothing. It's a good sketch, but the guy didn't give us much to go on."

Fran's shoulders drooped slightly. Then she pushed them back. "I'm sure it's something."

Stepping toward the table and motioning her to sit, he laid the folder down. "The guy might have been wearing a disguise. He has a beard, but it could be fake. He also has a hat and sunglasses on. We had hoped for more..." His voice trailed off. Taking a deep breath, he opened the folder and showed it to Mr. Montgomery first.

No recognition filled his eyes. Montgomery stared at the picture, examining it like a new piece of furniture getting ready for delivery. He moved the picture closer, examining it carefully, his eyes moving slowly over it.

"No." The word came in a hoarse whisper.

A moment longer and the picture changed to Ms. Fran's hands and gaze. She, too, studied the sketch. Terrence could see her willing herself to see something familiar, something that clued her in on this man's identity. Defeat came in the form of tears brimming in her eyes. She handed the picture back to Terrence and reached for Mr. Montgomery's hand. "I don't recognize him."

Terrence closed the folder. "It was a long shot. Like I said, the guy covered his face pretty well. It's really hard to recognize someone on so little."

He glanced at the now-wrinkled stack of papers on

the table. Luke and Ms. Fran didn't appear visibly upset or out of control, but he imagined the crinkled lists of names was a result of some emotions that had probably overflowed as they'd gone through them.

"How about the lists? Did you come up with anything?"

Ms. Fran glanced at Luke then handed Terrence the papers. "Nobody we think might be involved. We highlighted Julie's closest friends on each list."

Terrence took the papers and witnessed another exchanged look. He suspected his hunch about some deeper emotions exploding earlier were correct. They needed to let it out. There was no telling how long their search would last. Especially since every path they took turned out fruitless.

He glanced at the sheets. Two or three names glowed with yellow highlighter on each. "OK. Patterson and I will start interviewing from the marked names. Any advice on where to start?"

Mr. Montgomery and Ms. Fran exchanged a glance. She raised her eyebrows. He shrugged his shoulders.

"OK. How about where not to start? Who on the list might know the least?"

"Our church friends." Mr. Montgomery reached over and thumbed through until he found the right sheet. "They all came over last night and surely would have said something if they knew anything. You've already talked with Sue Teeter."

"I'll have someone touch base, but I'd like to focus somewhere more promising." He examined the lists.

Julie had moved to Williamsburg with her mom a couple years after finishing community college. It was possible that something had happened in Lynchburg no one had known about. If Julie didn't tell her husband about her abusive father and how she and Ms. Fran left, there might be something else she'd hidden. "College. I'll start with her college friends."

"Lynchburg. That'll take you about three hours." Ms. Fran interjected. "When will you go?"

"Now. Or at least as soon as I get together with my partner." He did some quick calculating. "By the time we grab what we need and get on the road, we'll probably arrive too late to do any interviews tonight. But we'll start first thing tomorrow." His phone buzzed. "Maybe that's Patterson now." He was wrong. He held up a finger and stepped into the living room. "Cooper here."

"Hi, Hon."

"Hey, Ma."

"You sound tired. How's the case going?"

"Slow."

"Are you eating?"

"Yes, Ma. I'm eating."

"When will I get to see my boy? How about this Sunday?"

He rolled his eyes. Church again. "I don't know. It all depends on this case. I've got to follow it through. I'm going to Lynchburg tonight."

"Sounds serious."

"It is."

"You be careful, son."

The picture of his petite mother holding a wooden spoon in her hand poised to give a much-deserved whooping popped into his mind. He might carry a Glock, but he wouldn't dare cross his ma. "I always am. I love you, and I'll call you soon."

"I love you, too."

Terrence turned. Ms. Fran stood in the doorway. How much had she heard? She probably thought him rude and unprofessional for taking a call from his mother. She held up her hand. "Hold on a sec." He covered the mouthpiece. "Ms. Fran?"

"That's your mother, right?"

"Yes, ma'am."

"I'd like to talk to her for a second, if I could. Mothers always like to hear what a blessing their children are to others. I want to thank the woman that raised such a good, thorough, compassionate detective."

He opened his mouth, but no words formed. Ms. Fran wanted to talk to his mother, not berate him for taking a personal call. His hand, apparently disconnected from his brain, stretched out to meet hers.

She accepted the thin phone. "Hi, is this Officer Cooper's mother?"

Ms. Fran smiled at the response.

"Yes, ma'am. We've been keeping your son quite busy. You've done a fine job. He's as polite and respectful an officer as I've ever met."

Silence from Ms. Fran's end plucked at his nerves. He should've put the phone on speaker. Or turned the volume up. His mother's boisterous voice would have crossed the three feet of air between him and Ms. Fran clearly.

"No. It's not easy raising a child by yourself. I raised my Julie alone, too." Tears filled Ms. Fran's eyes. "Yes. My Julie's missing. That's the case Terrence is working on. I know he wouldn't keep from seeing you otherwise."

He needed to cut this conversation off. Otherwise, his mother would blab all afternoon, and Ms. Fran would end up a wreck.

She raised the corner of her apron to dab a tear off each cheek. "Yes, I believe he will. Your Terrence will bring my Julie home." She smiled. "I'd love that."

Another pause. "It's a deal, then. When my Julie's home and Terrence wraps up the case, we'll get together."

He raised his eyebrows. A two-minute conversation and his mother had found a new friend. Unbelievable.

Hope once again took hold on Ms. Fran's face. "Your prayers are very welcome. OK. We'll talk then." Ms. Fran hung up the phone and handed it back to him. "Your mom's sweet."

"Yes, she is." He could think of nothing else to say.

"I guess you'd better get moving. Your mother says you'd better find my Julie quick so you can come by for supper."

Grinning, he pocketed his phone. "Yes, ma'am. I'll call tomorrow with an update."

He shook his head as he pulled out of the

driveway with the marked lists sitting on the seat beside him.

TWELVE

Fran curled up in her favorite chair and picked up her cup of steaming chocolate. Her company had all gone home. Julie and Luke's friends were so faithful in taking care of her. They'd brought the children this time, and Luke had spent most of the evening playing Candyland with Mattie, Heather and Craig's three-year-old.

At the door, they'd insisted Luke go home with them. He declined. Fran had invited Luke to stay with her. He resisted her offer as well, saying he felt closer to Julie in their home.

Taking another warm sip, Fran sensed both the closeness and emptiness of being in her home with Julie still missing. She imagined Luke opted for another run, sprinting for miles until he trudged back home and fell into another night of fitful sleep. Fran herself had nothing more to give. She'd baked, decorated, and chatted the day away. People came by, offering prayers, support, and meals that she stuck in the freezer. They flowed in and out of the house and helped keep her busy. But the knowledge of her daughter's disappearance never left.

She held the cup in both hands and closed her eyes. *I know, God. You're in control. Just keep reminding me.*

The phone rang and her eyes popped. Terrence had said he wouldn't have any information tonight. He would call the next day.

She set down the cup and lifted the phone off its base. The number didn't look familiar. The area code wasn't local. Julie? Maybe she'd gotten to a phone. Her heart raced.

"Hello?"

Silence greeted her. Maybe it was Julie, but she couldn't talk. Hope and fear filled her voice. "Hello? Is anyone there?"

"Fran."

The sound of Stuart's voice, like cold steel, shot through her body. She considered throwing the offensive object across the room. Shock glued it in her hand.

"Fran, don't hang up. Please."

OK, God. Even more? There's even more for me to bear? She breathed deep and slow.

"Are you still there?"

"Yes."

A sigh came over the line. "Good. I know I'm probably the last person on earth you want to talk to."

She held her response.

"I'll take that as a 'yes.' I know what's going on with Julia. The police came to see me last night, asking questions."

She stared at Julie's wedding portrait. She'd rehearsed more times than she could count what she'd say to Stuart if she ever had the chance. And now she found it hard to breathe. "Julie."

"That's right. She goes by Julie now. She's grown into such a beautiful woman. You must be very proud."

Fran forced herself to breathe. What if he'd seen Julie. Or contacted her. Surely Julie would have said something. Or perhaps not. She had to find out.

As if reading her thoughts, he continued. "I've seen her, Fran, but she doesn't know it. I haven't been stalking her or anything. I wanted to find my daughters and..." He cleared his throat. "I wanted to tell Julie I'm sorry. Sorry for everything I did to her. Everything I put her through. Making the two of you run."

Her nose and eyes burned. She had never let herself dream that Stuart would recognize the pain and torture he'd put their daughters through. Put her through.

"I'm sorry for hurting you, too, Fran." His voice softened. "I was wrong, and there's no excuse."

Her heart remained barred against his voice. Stuart had said he was sorry dozens of times, only to beat her again. She'd learned long ago that his words were cheap.

"I understand if you're skeptical. I don't blame you." He paused. "Could you please let me know, though, when they find Julie? I want to know she's OK.

Or have Luke call me if you don't want to. That's all I ask."

She didn't answer. He was asking too much of her.

"That's all. I just wanted to finally say how sorry I am. To let you know I'm concerned about Julie and would love to know when she's home safely."

Still, she remained silent, her mouth resembling cotton.

"Good-bye, Fran."

"No, wait." Her words came out more desperate than she wanted them to.

"Yes?"

"What happened? What changed?" She thought she'd forgiven Stuart long ago. Let go of her dark and ugly past with him. But hearing his voice, sensing a change, she wanted to know. Needed to know.

"I hit bottom, Fran. I drank myself into a pit with no one to share my life with and nowhere to go. Ironically, I ended up in rehab just outside Lynchburg."

She gasped. He'd been near Lynchburg. The same town she and Julie had lived for over a decade.

"Yes, I know you and Julia, um, Julie lived there, too. That's how I originally found you. When I got out. When I started my life over."

"How?"

"It wasn't hard. You used your mom's maiden name. Plus, Julie was in the paper so many times for her school achievements. I'd have recognized that smile no matter what name you gave her."

Realization settled on Fran. Stuart had known

where they were for years. He'd lived only miles away from them at one time. Yet he never tried to get to them. "You never contacted her?"

Another sigh. "No. You seemed happy. Both of you. One thing they encouraged me to do was to make amends except when it might cause more harm. I thought it might do you and Julie more damage if I came to you. Even to apologize."

"No, it–" She stopped herself.

She'd have lived the nightmare all over again before he got a word out. Just like when she'd had to retell the story to Terrence. Like the emotions that stole through her at the sound of his voice. He'd done something for their good. He'd stayed away.

"Thank you." Anger fled from Fran. Fear disintegrated. The man she'd been married to didn't exist anymore. Or, at least, it seemed that way. "So that's it? You got sober and everything changed?"

He laughed. "It wasn't quite that simple. I spent six months in jail. Six months in rehab. And a year building a new life. I found sobriety, I found God, and I found a godly wife."

Fran struggled to wrap her brain around everything he'd said. "You're married? Do you have...?"

"Yes. I'm married. Her name is Pauline. I have a stepdaughter, Darlene, and a daughter, Emma. She has Julie's eyes. And no, I've never laid a hand on any of them."

She sat back in her chair. She hadn't realized she'd been leaning forward. Her head spun.

"And I've found Rebecca."

Her hand flew to her chest. Julie missing. Rebecca found. "Rebecca?"

"Yes. I found you and Julie, and you were doing all right. Pauline helped me find Rebecca to see if we could do something to help her. Something to make up for–well, truly nothing will make up for what I did. But we wanted to see if she'd found the happiness you and Julie had. She lives up here in northern Virginia."

"Is she...is she happy? Is Rebecca OK?"

The sigh Stuart let out sounded like one of defeat. "She's not. She's so badly damaged and unwittingly making it worse for herself."

The memories of that last night with Rebecca flooded her once again. She didn't suspect Rebecca had much of a chance to make a good life for herself. "How bad is it?"

"Rebecca's made some bad choices. Nothing irreparable. We try to help her when we can."

He must not want to tell her the gritty details. *Oh, my dear Rebecca. Where are you? What's going on with you?*

"I...is there a way I can contact her?"

"I'm afraid not. She doesn't always have a phone, and when she does, she refuses to give me the number. Even blocks it when she calls. Although that's not very often."

"Oh." She swallowed. "I'll start praying for her more."

Somehow, knowing where Rebecca was and that she needed Fran increased the desperation for her oldest daughter. She'd never stopped praying for her, but there had always been a hope that she held onto. A hope that Rebecca had made good friends, found someone to take care of her and help guide her into adulthood.

She could no longer hold onto that slim thread of hope. She'd start sending up urgent prayers for the safety of both her daughters. But only one of them knew the Lord. She couldn't imagine life without Julie, but if she never came home, at least Fran knew Julie's eternal destination.

"That would be good. Know that Pauline and I and our friends are also praying." Stuart's voice lowered. "For Julie, too. You'll let me know?"

"Yes."

She hung up and eyed the phone left silent in her hand. Finding Rebecca. Receiving Stuart's sincere apology. These were the blessings in the storm.

Shaking her head, she replaced the phone on its charger and picked up her cup. The now cool liquid didn't soothe her as it had before. She set the cup back down and fingered the book beside it on the table. She hadn't picked up her Bible since learning of Julie's disappearance. She'd kept busy, prayed, and poured out her heart to God. She'd listened. But had yet to delve into His word.

Time to change that. She lifted the Bible and opened it to Psalms. She read until she couldn't hold her eyes open a moment longer.

~*~

Terrence pored over the information he and Patterson had spent the afternoon gathering. They had addresses, phone numbers, and places of employment for the handful of friends Mr. Montgomery and Ms. Fran had highlighted on the high school and college lists. Only three of them still lived in Lynchburg. They'd start with those. He debated which one to approach first, wishing it was obvious.

Behind him, Patterson lay in one of the hotel beds snoring. The man had been helpful, but Terrence had been the one to put extra effort toward finding the missing woman. Yet he couldn't figure out why.

He'd been drawn into the case. Was it because of the husband's desperation? Or the mother's kindness despite her fear. Or possibly both. He saw in Ms. Fran the things he loved about his own mother. Luke was the kind of husband he desired to be one day.

The laptop screen returned his glare. That he couldn't get a grip or a firm lead in this case confounded him to no end. He'd done nothing but spin his wheels for two days. Refocusing, he inspected the information before him. He clicked his way back into Julie's social media page and dug through post after post. He couldn't sleep, especially with the reverberating noise coming from the other bed, so he might as well keep looking for clues.

THIRTEEN

Terrence blinked against the blaring sunlight. The pounding of water from the hotel shower filtered through the bathroom door. Patterson, who'd slept soundly and thunderously, had gotten up at first light, flung open the blackout curtains, and whistled his way to the shower.

Growling, not ready to pop out of bed yet, Terrence covered his eyes with his arm. Hours of searching the night before had produced nothing. Like the fig tree with leaves but no fruit, each turn or promising lead proved empty.

Where had that come from?

Guess some of the Bible stories drilled into him from infancy had stuck.

Cocking his right ankle on his left knee, he forced his mind back to the case at hand. Julie Montgomery had been missing for forty-eight hours, and he had no solid lead. For her sake, he hoped the day ahead would produce something. Anything that would clue them into why a happy, contented wife had disappeared.

If only the woman hadn't been so secretive. If she hadn't told her husband about an abusive past with her father, she may have taken other secrets with her. He hoped they'd be able to figure them out.

The shower shut off. Patterson's humming came through the cheap door. Terrence groaned and pushed himself to a sitting position on the side of the bed. The hotel room looked like a million others. Indiscriminate carpet, thick, dark curtains on one end of the room, sink and mirror flanked by the bathroom door on one side and an open closet on the other.

Coffee. He needed coffee. Spotting the small pot on top of the refrigerator, he filled it, placed the pre-measured filter bag in its slot, and had just clicked the switch to *on* when Patterson stepped out of the bathroom. He wore his blue uniform slacks and a bright smile. Terrence rolled his eyes.

"Mornin'."

He grunted.

Patterson's smile widened. "Late night?"

"You could say that." The coffee dripped into the pot too slowly.

"Find anything?" Patterson stuck a toothbrush in his mouth.

"No. Nothing other than some more info on the highlighted friends of Mrs. Montgomery. At least we won't have to waste time this morning tracking them down."

"Humph."

Terrence cupped a hand over his ear.

Patterson spit foamed toothpaste into the sink.

"That's good."

Hoping the pot had an automatic switch that shut off the drip when the pot went missing, he yanked it out and poured a cup. He sipped the hot, black liquid, willing the caffeine to metabolize quickly. "Hopefully one of the three locals will know something helpful. One friend moved to Tennessee, the last is military. Most recent address, Ft. Benning, Georgia."

Now fully dressed, Patterson walked to the coffeepot and poured himself a cup. He doctored it and took a sip. "I don't know. I wouldn't mind going south this time of year."

Terrence drained his coffee. "That won't do Julie Montgomery any good for us to spend more time chasing empty rabbit holes. I'm gonna take a shower."

The caffeine and hot water combined to refresh him some. Two more cups and he'd be equipped to tackle the day. He and Patterson were both ready twenty minutes after seven. "Let's get some breakfast, and then we'll call the first one, Colleen White. She's an elementary teacher and shouldn't leave home 'til after eight."

"Continental or IHOP?"

"IHOP. It might be a long day. I'd like to start it with some real sustenance." They had spotted the breakfast hotspot two blocks from the hotel. Therefore, getting to the restaurant wouldn't eat up much time. The school where Ms. White taught was only fifteen minutes away and her home slightly off the straight path between them and the school. Wherever she met them, they could be face-to-face by eight thirty.

Half an hour later, Terrence pushed back the empty plate which had held pancakes, sausage, eggs, and grits. A pool of syrup was the only evidence of the scarfed food. He checked his notes and dialed their first contact's number.

"Hello?" answered a bubbly voice.

Good grief. Cheerful people first thing in the morning. "Good morning, Ms. White. My name is Officer Cooper from Williamsburg."

"Yes?" The exuberance toned down a bit.

"My partner and I are in town doing some research on Julie Montgomery. We know you were friends and wondered if we could steal a few minutes of your time this morning to ask you a few questions."

"Julie?"

"Yes, ma'am. It's an urgent matter, and we'd like to speak to you right away."

"Is she OK?"

"That's what we're trying to find out. We'll tell you more in person. Where's a good place to meet you in twenty minutes?"

"My, um..." Colleen hesitated. He must've thrown her off kilter. She surprised him when she continued with renewed liveliness in her voice. "My classroom at school. I teach at—"

"Yes, ma'am. I know where the school is. We'll meet you there."

He clicked the phone off, threw a tip on the table, and headed to the cashier. Eighteen minutes later he and Patterson checked in as guests at Hillside Elementary School and were directed to Colleen

White's classroom.

Standing at the door, they waited for the tall, blonde standing behind the desk to finish a conversation with whom Terrence assumed was a fellow teacher. Her animated voice matched her hands, which punctuated every other word.

When she spotted them in the doorway, her voice trailed off and her hands suspended midair. The other teacher, older and slightly gray, although as thin as Colleen, excused herself and slipped out the door past them.

Terrence strode across the tiled floor into the desk-littered, brightly decorated room and held his hand out. "Ms. White, I'm Officer Terrence Cooper." He nodded at Patterson, who'd stepped up to shake hands as well. "This is my partner, Officer Patterson."

She stood awkwardly by her desk. "I don't understand. I haven't talked to Julie in years. Except once in a while on Facebook."

"Have a seat, Ms. White." Patterson dragged two metal-legged, pint-sized chairs to face the desk. He sat in one and Terrence, seeing no better alternative, took the other. "We're sorry to spring this on you, but the matter is urgent."

"The matter?" She arched her finely trimmed eyebrows.

Clearing his throat, Patterson looked to Terrence to bear the bad news.

"Ms. White, two days ago, Julie Montgomery disappeared on her way to work. We're trying to find her."

Her mouth dropped open and her hands flew up to cover it, her eyes rounded until they bulged. "Disappeared? Julie's missing?"

"Yes, ma'am. Nothing has turned up as a lead so far."

Colleen's hands fell to her lap. "I don't understand what I can do. I told you I haven't talked to Julie in years. Just comments and likes on the computer."

Patterson leaned forward. "I understand this comes as a shock, Ms. White. The thing is, we don't have any clues as to what might have happened. Nothing in her life now seems to be related to her disappearance. We understand you were good friends at one time. We thought you might know something about Julie's past life. When she was in high school or college here before she moved."

Hands shaking, she raised them in question. "I don't know. Julie was nice. We were on the cheerleading squad in high school. We did a lot of things together but weren't exactly close." Her eyes glazed over as if remembering. "I liked Julie. We all did. But she never opened up. Never told secrets to us. She always listened. Julie was a great shoulder to cry on. But she never once cried on our shoulders. We admired her strength, but it's hard to really get to know someone so quiet about her own life."

Terrence swallowed frustration. Again, nothing. Another perfect, in-control, closed-off description of Julie Montgomery.

"Is there nothing you can think of?" Either Patterson didn't feel the same frustration, or he hid it better than Terrence. "Not necessarily something Julie said, but something she did? Or someone around her. A boyfriend?"

Colleen tapped the side of her nose. "I don't know..." She pushed back her chair and walked to the fish tank sitting on a table under a window. "That was a long time ago."

Terrence met Patterson's gaze. He doubted she had any useful information.

Drumming her fingers on the top edge of the tank, she stood still as time ticked. Suddenly, she turned on her heels. Grace exuded from her pores even in stress.

He opened his mouth to thank her for her time.

"There was a boyfriend."

He snapped his mouth shut and leaned forward. "Anything about him? Did he seem possessive? Try to monopolize Julie's time?"

She strode to her chair and sat back down. Elbows propped on the desk, she shook her head. "I don't think so. They started dating our senior year, after football season finished. We didn't usually see Julie much during off-season."

"Do you remember his name?"

Colleen tapped the side of her nose again. "Toby...Turner...Terry...something like that."

Terrence leaned in. "Do you remember what he looked like? Dark hair, light hair? Did he keep a mustache? A goatee? "

Anguish took over her features. "I don't know. It was high school. I was busy having fun. Julie didn't party much. I want to help, I do. I just don't remember."

Reaching forward, Patterson laid a comforting hand on Colleen's forearm. "It's OK. We know you want to help Julie." He handed her a card and stood. "If you think of anything, a name, a face, a memory that doesn't seem right, give me a call."

"I will." She slipped the card into her top desk drawer and glanced at the digital clock over the door leading to the hallway. "I'm really sorry I couldn't help."

"It's OK. Every little bit helps. We better get out of your hair and let you prepare for your students." Patterson slid the chairs back to their homes and followed Terrence out of the room.

Brooding, Terrence remained silent through signing out on the visitor log and on the walk across the now-buzzing parking lot. Bouncing students with backpacks slung over thick coats and chatting parents milled everywhere. Normalcy. Most people reveled in it. Terrence gritted his teeth. He saw people's lives when normalcy flew out the window. Not a soul on this campus other than Colleen White had an idea that a woman had gone missing and had an unknown fate. Would it change their day for longer than a minute if they knew? Probably not.

He slid into the driver's seat with a huff and programmed the GPS with the next address on his list.

"Where to now?"

"Darla Compton. She and Julie went to community college together. Works as a CPA across town."

"Want me to make the call?"

"Sure. Thanks." He pushed the notepad toward Patterson, who flipped his phone open and dialed.

"Darla Compton, please."

Terrence cranked the engine and inched out of the parking space. He crept out of the lot and down the short drive to the main road. Buses flooded in from the opposite direction. Patterson ended the call.

"Well?"

"She's in, but she was on the other line. Guess in person's a better way to break the news, anyway."

"Guess so. At least we know she's there." Terrence turned left and continued to follow the directions of the GPS to Willis and Dunbar CPA Firm.

FOURTEEN

Terrence's aggravation hadn't decreased by the time he steered the car into the parking lot adjacent to the two-story brick building labeled 'Willis and Dunbar.' They had crossed paths with several school buses still picking up students and had traversed two school zones as they wove their way through Lynchburg. Patterson must have seen the steam coming off Terrence and decided best not to make small talk on the ride over. The only thing penetrating the silence was the mechanized voice from the GPS guiding their way.

Without uttering a word, Terrence exited the car and headed toward the double glass doors. Patterson eased up beside him at the receptionist's desk. The middle-aged woman had a pretty face and jet black hair. She held up one pudgy finger and continued talking into the microphone on the headset she wore.

"Of course. I understand." She doodled on a business notepad beside the phone. "Yes, ma'am. Mr. Willis is aware of the situation."

Terrence drummed his fingers on the high part of the desk that held a bowl of mints and some financial flyers.

"Yes. He'll get to it as soon as possible and get back with you right away." More doodling. "Sure. No problem. OK. Bye-bye." Hanging up the phone, the receptionist smiled warmly at the two uniformed officers. "Good morning. Welcome to Willis and Dunbar. How may I help you?"

Terrence flashed his I.D. "I'm Officer Cooper." He motioned toward his partner, who also flashed his shield. "This is Officer Patterson. We'd like to meet with Ms. Darla Compton."

The receptionist's mouth formed an "O" and she furrowed her eyebrows. "Do you have an appointment?"

"No. We're here on official business."

"I'm sorry. Miss Compton's at a seminar in Blackstone. She's actually teaching it."

Steepling his fingers on the desk, Terrence looked at her hard. "We called only a little while ago and was told she was here."

The woman shifted in her chair. "I'm sorry. Miss Compton came in but left about twenty minutes ago. Do you need to see her right away?" Her face showed a struggle between helping the officers and disturbing one of her bosses.

Terrence calculated how far ahead she was. Trying to catch up with her wouldn't be worth the effort.

Patterson leaned in and looked at Terrence. "We have one more contact, right?"

Terrence barely nodded.

Patterson turned to the receptionist. "We can come back. What time will Miss Compton return?"

Relief relaxed the worry lines on the receptionist's face, and her fingers flew on the keyboard. "Um, the seminar ends at one. She'll be back around two."

Smiling, Patterson thanked her. "Good enough. We'll be back then."

Terrence glared at the back of Patterson's head as he followed him out. Once shut in the car, Terrence turned on him. "Why in the world did you do that? Now we have to kill almost five hours."

Patterson shrugged his shoulders. "Who wants to take that drive for no reason? We do have another contact to interview. And besides, there's no guarantee she'll have any helpful information."

Pounding a fist on the steering wheel, Terrence spoke through clenched teeth. "Time. We're wasting time. And you don't even seem to care. Does it even matter to you that a woman's missing?"

"Of course I care. But it doesn't do the investigation any good to lose my temper." His eyes narrowed. "You sure didn't care about this case when it first came your way."

"That's when a woman had been missing for two hours. Now she's been missing for two days. Big difference."

Turning to stare out the windshield, Patterson sat motionless. "Fine. You're right. I could be more time conscious. But you could afford to be less hot-headed. What's done is done. Who's next?"

Terrence and Patterson tracked down Amber Fitch at the construction office where she worked. She knew as little information as Colleen White. Their last hope for information today lay with Darla Compton, and she wouldn't be available for hours yet. Might as well get some lunch. Terrence opted for take-out and headed back to the hotel room. Patterson skipped the fast food and strode over to the hometown burger joint a few doors down from the hotel.

After wolfing down a spicy chicken sandwich, fries, and soda, Terrence tried to take a nap. Sleep refused to come. He changed clothes and headed to the hotel gym. An hour later, his heart pumped with the satisfaction of exercising every muscle he could get to. His mood lightened with the exertion, and he met Patterson's glance with a nod as he entered the room. By the time he'd taken a shower, the time arrived to head back to Willis and Dunbar.

The raven-haired receptionist greeted them with the same smile as before. "Hi. Miss Compton is in her office. Second floor, third door on the right after you get off the elevator. She's expecting you."

Courteous and efficient. Terrence nodded his appreciation. "Thank you."

Moments later, he rapped on the door with Darla Compton's name on it. A faint "Come in" filtered through the door.

Behind a large oak desk sat a serious looking woman in a dark blue suit. Darla Compton's sandy-blond hair was pulled back into a tight bun. She adjusted the thin, wire-rimmed glasses sitting on the bridge of her nose. "Please sit down, officers."

Terrence took the chair on the left. "We're here, Miss Compton, to ask you some questions about Julie Montgomery."

Her face remained expressionless. "Julie?"

"Yes, ma'am. We understand you went to community college together?"

"We did."

Glancing at Patterson, Terrence continued. "Two days ago, Mrs. Montgomery vanished, and we're looking into all her close relationships."

Miss Compton's eyes widened. "Disappeared?"

"Yes. We're looking for a solid lead that might help us find her."

"I'm not sure how I can help. Julie and I were close once, but that was years ago. I saw her at her wedding last month, but before then we hadn't seen each other since she moved to Williamsburg."

Patterson leaned forward. "We understand Mrs. Montgomery was a very quiet person and severed most connections when she moved. What we're looking for is something, maybe someone, or an incident that happened in the past that might clue us into her disappearance."

"Something in her past?"

"Yes. We understand she began dating a guy in high school, but no one seems to know much about him."

"Todd? Yeah, I remember him." Miss Compton pursed her lips then continued, "We double dated a few times. He never said much, but I didn't get the warm fuzzies from him."

"Did he and Julie have a tumultuous relationship?"

"Not that I know of." Miss Compton's hand rose to her right ear and she played with the diamond stud adorning it. "She talked about him all the time but didn't bring him around much. I almost got the feeling he didn't like going out when a group of us got together. They usually went out alone or stayed in at his place."

Terrence and Patterson exchanged glances. Pulling out his notebook and pen, Terrence took over questioning. "You said his name is Todd. Todd what?"

"Um...Adams, I think. Yes, that's right. Todd Adams."

"And he lived here in Lynchburg, too?"

"Yes." The fidgeting hand dropped, and Darla Compton laced her fingers together on her desk.

"Sounds like he might have been a little possessive." They might be getting somewhere.

Lips pursed again, Miss Compton seemed to mull over the statement before answering. "I guess I never thought about it at the time. Plus, I finished my degree in Blacksburg, so I wasn't around for a couple years. But, yeah, I guess. He didn't like other people being around."

Terrence tapped his pen on the notebook. "Anything else? Do you think it ever crossed into something more than being possessive?"

"Not that I–" Her face froze, then her lips parted as if she had something to say.

"Miss Compton?"

"Well, I...It could be nothing."

Terrence leaned forward. "Or it could be everything. What do you remember?"

"Julie was a private person. Not open like most of my girlfriends. She never went to the bathroom with the girls or anything." Her face flushed. "But one time, I was at her house getting ready to go out. I had to use the restroom, and she was in the shower. When I opened the door, she'd just gotten out. A bruise poked out of the top of the towel on her back and I swear I saw fingerprints on her upper arm. She swore it was nothing, that she and Todd had been wresting and she'd bumped into a table."

"Did you believe her?"

"No, not really. But what could I say? I never saw anything else, and she never mentioned it again."

Holding himself in his seat, Terrence continued. "And this Todd Adams. He's the same guy she dated in high school?"

"Yeah. They dated for like four years. Right up until she moved."

"Until she left?"

"Uh huh. She broke up with him the day before."

Planned it. She escaped, just like her mother had years before.

He stood and held out his hand. "Thank you, Miss Compton. You've been more helpful than you know." Patterson followed suit.

Miss Compton's nose crinkled.

"What is it?"

"He called me and asked about Julie."

"He called you?" Terrence asked.

"Yeah. I didn't think anything about it back then. He was upset. His girlfriend had dumped him and moved away."

Terrence held her gaze. "What'd you tell him?"

Miss Compton shrugged. "I didn't know anything. Julie never told me where she and her mom were moving. It was a couple years later before we reconnected online, and I found out she'd moved to Williamsburg."

Terrence studied the woman in her perfectly tailored suit with hair swept up with nary a strand out of place. What secrets did she hold? No more about Julie Montgomery, he surmised. He nodded. "Thank you."

The first flicker of concern filtrated Darla Compton's composure, turning the edges of her lips down. "Do you think Julie's OK? Did Todd have something to do with her disappearance?"

"Those are the exact questions we intend to answer."

Patterson rushed to keep up with Terrence as he sprinted through the building and out to the car. "What now? We don't have any information on this guy. You can't go barreling around looking for him."

"We get information. We'll go back to the hotel and get what we can off the computer. Put a call in to Clark and have him pull up what he can from the office. Adams is a pretty common name, but Lynchburg's not that big."

FIFTEEN

Julie opened her eyes, her heart racing. She took in the sparsely-decorated room, sighed, and closed them again.

She'd been dreaming about Luke. He held her tight in his arms until she fell asleep. In her dream, she'd nestled against him and played with the little tuft of hair on his chest. They talked about the future, the children they'd have, what they would name them, and how they would decorate the two tiny bedrooms that now sat empty.

Then Julie had smelled smoke. In her dream, their house caught fire, starting suddenly from a night light in a room decorated for a baby girl. After she opened her eyes, she realized real smoke billowed from the wood-burning stove in the adjoining room.

A tear slid down her cheek. She didn't know which was worse. Being in the dream and having her house burn down or waking up to the continuing real nightmare.

Be strong and courageous. I am with you wherever you go.

Holding tight to the words, Julie shut her eyes and rolled to her side. He had relaxed on the tethers, and she now only had her left hand strapped to the bedpost. *Only.* She snorted. Just one arm tied down. It was crazy. Pure lunacy. She couldn't see how any of it could fit into God's perfect plan for her.

Faith when everything's going the way you want is easy. When your world is falling apart, when it's hard to trust, and faith is maintained, that's how we know if we truly trust God.

Their pastor said those words in a sermon a couple years back. His wife had been diagnosed with pancreatic cancer. Still, they believed.

She died four months later. Still, he believed.

OK, God. I know You're here with me. Even in the middle of this craziness.

Pushing herself to a sitting position, Julie dug into the knot around her wrist with her free fingers. Unsuccessful again, she laid her head back. Exhaustion provided a strong gravitational pull on all her muscles. Her lack of energy could be due to being strapped to the bed and not being able to move freely. Or the stress and fear. Or something else. She needed to–

"Good morning, sunshine." He stood at the door, grinning like she'd invited him in. "I have your breakfast. Scrambled eggs, soft, and toast with strawberry jelly. Just the way you like it."

Bile rose in her throat, and she swallowed it down. She couldn't make him angry. She needed to keep things calm. He seemed to be in a decent mood this morning and, she needed to keep him that way.

No words came to her, so she turned and dropped her legs off the side of the bed in a seated position. He pulled the tray over and sat the plate down. "I'll be right back. The coffee's about finished perking."

She hoped the toast would help calm her stomach. Julie was working on her second slow bite when he came in the room carrying a steaming cup of coffee.

"Two creams, three sugars." He sat the cup down triumphantly and pulled a metal folding chair over from the wall.

Julie tried a bite of egg. He stared as she chewed the mushy protein. Watching her eat couldn't be that interesting. She swallowed.

"What's wrong?" The words pierced her thoughts, which were waffling between the contradiction of wanting to focus on trusting God and the reality of her situation.

"Wrong?"

He leaned toward her and propped his elbows on the tray. Dark gray eyes bore into her. "Yes. What's wrong? You've hardly eaten a thing since we've been here, and you sleep all the time."

The words acted like a vacuum, sucking out all her other thoughts. The egg in her mouth turned to slime. She swallowed it along with the fear in her throat. "Why am I here?"

His eyes narrowed to slits. "You're here because you're mine. You always were. You always will be. I told you that before. I keep my word."

Rage, not fear, rose in Julie. Cheeks hot and hands shaking, her gaze didn't waver from his. "You can keep me tied here." She waved her secured arm. "But you can't make me like it or be OK with it. Nor can you make me yours again."

She snatched up the plate of barely touched food with her free hand and flung it across the room. *So much for keeping things calm.*

He shoved the folding chair back and the shaking moved from Julie's hands to the rest of her body.

Strong hands framed Julie's face, palms on her cheeks and fingers clamped on her temples. Pressure building, he leaned in until his hot, pungent breath brushed her face. "You are mine. Get it through your thick skull before I have to force it in."

"Never."

"We'll see about that."

She waited for the first blow. It never came. He abruptly let go and stormed out of the room, slamming the door behind him.

She fell back onto the bed, trembling head to toe. Her own strength surprised her. She'd never crossed him before, never stood up to him. God had to be the source. The strength and courage He talked about.

Julie had always been so careful. Measuring every word, every movement, every look, hoping not to set him off. The slightest thing would send him into a rage without warning.

Even when she broke up and ran from him, she didn't do it to his face. Everything had been planned to the tiniest detail. The job applications. The interview.

The new house. Making excuses why he couldn't come over for two weeks as she and her mom packed. Texting him from the hotel she stayed at the night before the movers picked up the boxes. She'd never been strong to his face. She'd simply left.

Turning her head, she spotted the mug of coffee left on the tray. Her morning cup of coffee. Would she ever kiss Luke good-bye as she headed for work and stop at her favorite drive-thru for a tall nonfat latte again?

Don't lose hope.

She had to believe she'd get back home. Back to Luke and her mom. Back to normal and sane.

The rumbling of Julie's stomach brought her back to the present. She needed to get to the restroom. The nausea had resulted in her throwing up only once, but that didn't mean it wouldn't again. The long rope allowed her to move around on the bed and even walk to the end of it, but not get to the bathroom. He wanted to monitor everything. Be in control of her every second.

Despite herself and her full bladder, Julie's mouth watered for that coffee. The tepid liquid did nothing more than moisten her tongue but didn't warm her up. Didn't spark fond memories. Nor did it calm her stomach.

She sank down to the edge of the bed, plunked her elbows on her knees, and buried her face in her hands. There had to be a way out.

~*~

He opened the door and leaned against the frame. "So you need me now?"

Heat rose to Julie's cheeks. She didn't know how long she'd dozed off, but the pressure from her bladder had awakened her. She couldn't put off calling for him any longer. "I need to go to the bathroom."

"Fine."

Julie stood by the bed after he untied her.

"Well?"

She looked at the dresser, where she'd stored her supplies from the day before.

This time, his cheeks reddened. "Oh. Fine. I'll shut the door. You can't get out of here anyway." He patted the back of his waistband. "I have my little friend. I don't want to hurt you, but I'll do what it takes to make you understand."

The door clicked, and Julie rushed to the dresser, taking out one package and the box she'd bought. She closed the bathroom door, wishing there was a lock.

He wouldn't dare come in. He'd be too grossed out.

Allowing a smile to penetrate her nerves, she opened both items. The contents of the box quivered in her hand. She set it aside and took a pad out of the package. She didn't want any suspicion to arise if he decided to check behind her and make sure she'd been telling the truth.

She finished up and washed her hands slowly,

thoroughly, keeping her eyes trained on them. She dried her hands, making sure to get every speck of water between each finger and underneath each neatly trimmed fingernail. Closing her eyes, she took a deep breath before opening them and looking at the little stick on the sink.

Two pink lines stared back at her. She couldn't believe this was happening now.

Joy and fear washed over her. A baby. The baby she and Luke had talked about, planned for, desperately desired. A baby.

Picking up the pregnancy test and staring at it, she shook all over. She and Luke had decided not to do anything to prevent pregnancy from the very beginning. His mother had tried years before having him. They had no idea how long it would take, and they figured God would be in control anyway.

Are You? Are You really in control in this, God? Her hands cupped her still-flat stomach. A tiny baby thrived and grew there. She had to protect herself for her baby's sake. For her and Luke's baby. She'd bite her tongue. She'd listen for God's voice. She'd do whatever it took to get through this until someone found her or she figured a way out.

"Aren't you done yet?" The irritated voice pushed its way into the only private space she'd been able to create.

"Finishing up." Julie slipped the pregnancy test back in the box, left the other package by the toilet in case he checked it, and slipped into the bedroom. She placed the box back in the top drawer of the dresser.

She had no way to hide it. She simply had to hope his squeamishness kept him out of that drawer. Moving back by the bed she called out, "OK."

The door opened. "Took long enough. You women and the bathroom. I'll never understand the fascination with being in there." He tied her back to the bed, held her gaze for what felt like five minutes, then left the room. The door remained open.

At least she'd get some heat, now. She laid on her left side and let her hands rest on her stomach.

I'm pregnant. The words flooded her with more emotion than she could have ever imagined.

SIXTEEN

Back at the hotel, Terrence set up his laptop. He dug into finding Todd Adams' personal information while Patterson scanned the web on his own computer for any articles or data on the guy. He'd called Clark back at the office on the way and tasked him with searching the state and district databases to see if Adams had ever been in the system.

Having scribbled down Adams' current and past two addresses, Terrence moved on to DMV and scoped out his vehicle make, model, and license plate number. He made his way into driving records but didn't find much. A few speeding tickets and one reckless driving over the last seven years. Pretty typical for a young, twenty-something hot-shot kid.

Leaning back in the stiff, barely cushioned chair, Terrence glanced at Patterson, who'd set up on the bed. "How're you coming over there?"

Patterson looked up. "Haven't found anything so far. He doesn't have a social media page, nor did I find him on any of the other networking sights. No articles in the paper mention him in the last year. I'm digging farther back now."

"OK. I wonder what's taking Clark so long?"

"Who knows? Maybe something came up."

Terrence tapped his pen on his pad. "No. He knows this is top priority. There are plenty of others to catch whatever calls come in."

Shrugging, Patterson returned his gaze to the laptop in front of him. "He could be having trouble finding information."

"I hope–" Terrence's cellphone rang. He checked the caller I.D. and gave a curt nod Patterson's direction before hitting accept. "Whatcha got?"

"I've got a whole lot. I just sent you an e-mail with the records I've found so far. This guy seems to have been flying right under the radar for some time. Not quite far enough, though. The details are in the files, but I'll give you the skinny."

Terrence wove his way through the right pages on the screen in front of him to get to his e-mail, clicked on the most current one from Clark, and skimmed through as he continued.

"Todd Adams was a foster kid, taken from his home at age ten. I won't tell you what the file looks like. It's in the e-mail."

Terrence opened the attachment labeled "CPS." A low whistle escaped. Fifty-three pages. A thick file was never good.

"He made it through high school then became a mechanic. I've included his most recent recorded place of employment. He's had no problems there that I can find, but it's the seventh place he's worked in the last nine years. I'd wager that means he's been trouble or has conflict with authority."

Terrence clicked open files. "Uh huh."

"There're only a couple convictions as an adult, related to the same incident. A drunk in public and an assault and battery. He got into a fight at a bar about four years back and left the other guy missing a few teeth and cracked a few ribs."

"Nice."

"Exactly. If this is your guy, and my instinct says it is, he's got a temper and doesn't mind putting some oomph behind it."

Terrence ended the call, leaned back in the chair, and closed his eyes against the bombardment of material, trying to organize and file the summary of information in his mind.

Opening his eyes, he rifled through the paperwork in the folder he'd been carrying for the last few days and pulled out the picture of Julie Montgomery in her eighteenth century work costume. This woman, who'd lived a seemingly perfect life, had hidden a most terrible secret. She had, however, done the right thing. She'd left her abuser, moved away, and cut all ties, not leaving herself open to being drawn back in.

She'd messed up, too. She'd created a neat and organized life because of the chaos she'd experienced as a child. Those early tendencies had most likely been exacerbated with the abuse he now suspected she'd suffered for years at the hands of Todd Adams. Becoming almost ritualistic in the way she lived her life had left Julie Montgomery vulnerable, making herself an easy target.

He shook his head. However Adams had learned of Julie's whereabouts, it most likely didn't take him long to track her and figure out the best time, place, and method to snatch her. He shoved the picture back into the file and read the scores of pages laid out in front of him on the screen.

Two hours later, he pushed back the chair, stood up, and stretched. The rolling of his head shoulder to shoulder and chest to back did little to relieve the tension in his neck. The dryness in his eyes had crossed the line of burning to feeling like sandpaper lined his eyelids every time he blinked. Ignoring Patterson's gaze, he strolled to the bathroom vanity and dropped several drips of moisturizing relief in each eye. He also ignored his growling stomach.

"So?"

Terrence continued to work on the stiffness in his neck. "It's ugly. Abusive doesn't begin to describe the home this kid grew up in. He had cigarette burn marks on his chest, arms, and thighs, and evidence of at least six broken bones that had healed, and signs he'd been molested. Child Protective Services took him from his parents when he was ten. Then he foster home hopped until he aged out. His social worker said mostly good things about him, attributing the trouble he ran into to his poor beginning." He shook his head. "I'm guessing he was pretty good about putting on a show when he needed to. He barely passed high school, where he obtained a thick record."

Pacing as he talked, Terrence also retraced the reports for himself. Knowing who he'd come up against and what they were capable of held utmost importance. "I'm guessing there's plenty not in the file. He got caught with a knife at one school. That caused an expulsion and a transfer to a different home. One foster parent said their family couldn't keep him because he scared the smaller kids in the house. The problems go on and on."

Patterson closed his computer. "I found a reference to a bar brawl."

"Yeah, lovely. He pled no contest and got probation and court ordered twelve step meetings." Terrence held his balled fists by his sides. He'd love to get this guy in a ring one on one and show him what it felt like to go up against a sober man instead of a girl or a guy weakened by too much alcohol. "He didn't need twelve step meetings. He needed cold, hard time locked away from society and innocent women like Julie."

"Looks like he might get it," Patterson interjected.

He cut his eyes to his unwanted partner. No nonchalance of the last couple of days showed on his face. Only determination emanated from his new partner's steady gaze and firm jaw. "Yeah. Now we have to catch him and haul him off without Julie Montgomery getting hurt."

"So what's the strategy?"

The pacing began again. Terrence had run over the options in his mind dozens of times. They were out of district. Time spent going through the hoops to get a search warrant would be just that–time spent. If someone at his residence let them in, though. He stopped and turned. "We go knock on his door."

Patterson let out a bitter laugh. "You do believe in direct, don't you?"

"Clark's good. He got the down low on Adams' roommate, too. They're both on the lease of the subsidized apartment they share. If this character really has her, what are the chances he's at home? But his loser roommate cashing in disability checks most likely is."

Patterson crossed his arms. "You're serious."

"Of course I am. Do I ever kid?" He ignored the look Patterson shot him. "This strung-out guy's going to be so glad we're not there for him, he'll give us whatever we want. Perry O'Brien. Three DUI's, no driver's license, receives disability for a work accident that messed up his back, and the cherry on top? Possession of cocaine. He'll freak when we show up, then roll out the welcome mat when we mention Adams' name."

"And if he doesn't?"

How did Patterson ever solve a case being so conservative? He did well at interviews, but his hesitancy to act caused Terrence more than a little trepidation about going into the unknown with him. "Then we'll deal with it. Hit the local station and push for a warrant until we get it. You know this is our guy, and given the information we've found, Julie Montgomery's already on borrowed time."

Patterson's feet hit the floor. "All right. But we

don't push O'Brien." He picked up his gear.

Terrence did likewise. "No problem. We'll just sweet talk our way in."

~*~

The apartment door tagged 415 had paint chipping and several dents. Terrence knocked. A stringy-haired, glazed-eyed guy opened it a moment later.

Adrenaline coursed through Terrence's veins, and he mustered every ounce of control not to push past him.

Perry's glossy eyes grew round, and he took a step back. "What–?"

Terrence took the lead. "Mr. O'Brien, we're here to see Todd Adams and ask him some questions." Might as well put the guy at ease as quickly as possible.

Relief washed over Perry O'Brien's face. "Uh, he's not here."

Of course he wasn't. "He lives here, right?"

"Yeah."

"So, is he out to dinner?" Terrence leaned against the doorjamb, feigning nonchalance.

"Nope." Perry shrugged. "Said he was goin' on a huntin' trip. Ain't never seen him hunt, but that's what he said."

Hunting trip. Terrence suppressed the shudder that coursed through him. "How long's he gone for?"

Cocking his head to one side, Perry shrugged again. "Don't know. He said a week or two. Don't really care. He left January's rent."

He darted his eyes to Patterson. The guy had been planning this for a while. Terrence let his shoulders slump. "Hmmm. We really need to ask him some questions. Do you know where he went on this hunting trip?"

The druggy's face remained blank. "Nope. Don't really care."

"Well, maybe he left some information about where he is…" Terrence tilted his head. "Mind if we come in and take a look at his room?"

Perry straightened. His face blanched. "I don't know…"

Terrence maintained his relaxed stance. "We're kind of in a hurry to talk to Todd. We just want to check out his room. We're not interested in anything else. Won't even have a chance to so much as take a glance at anything outside his bedroom." He'd already spotted the bag of weed amidst the food cartons, empty glasses, car magazines, and beer bottles on the coffee table.

"Yeah?"

"Yeah."

Perry stepped back. "I guess that'd be OK."

Pushing off the doorjamb, Terrence didn't give him a second to change his mind. They had their invitation in. "Thanks. Which room's his?"

He and Patterson followed Perry's pointed finger to a closed door down a short hallway. Terrence tried the handle and found it unlocked. Opening the door and flicking on a light revealed almost as much mess as they'd passed through in the tiny living room. An unmade double bed took up most of the floor space. A computer sat on a desk next to the bed. Stacks of paper and an empty plate filled the rest of the space on the desk. A chair and dresser finished the furniture count in the sparsely decorated room.

Terrence and Patterson donned thin latex gloves, and Terrence directed Patterson to the dresser while he tackled the computer and desk. A first riffling turned up nothing.

"Hey, look at this."

Terrence spun in the chair. Patterson held a picture frame he'd pulled out of the top drawer. A photo-shopped picture of Julie in her wedding dress had been placed in it. Todd Adams had added himself into her smiling picture.

Terrence squinted. "Don't remove anything. Take a photo of it with your phone and put it back where it was." He turned back to his task then swiveled back to Patterson. "Wait a minute. Let me see that."

Terrence accepted the picture from Patterson and pulled out his notebook. He plucked out the sketch of the guy the waitress at Colonial Williamsburg had seen with Julie Tuesday morning. He compared the crudely edited picture to the sketch then held it up. "What d'ya think?"

Patterson leaned in, his eyes scanning the two pages. "He did a good job of covering himself up. But I'm sure it's him."

"Me, too. Have Clark run the two pictures on the photo recognition software. There's a slim chance since this one's a profile, but worth a check."

Patterson snapped a photo then tapped away on his phone. "Done."

Focused back on the computer screen, Terrence continued his search. "OK, Todd. Where did you take Julie Montgomery?"

Papers and receipts littered the desk. Credit card, phone, electric, and insurance bills made up most of the pile. Great filing system. The top drawer produced ATM receipts, gas receipts, and a conglomeration of candy, empty wrappers, and pens. The second drawer was deep enough to have standing, hanging files, but everything inside it lay askew. A few papers down, Terrence hit pay dirt. A copy of Julie's wedding announcement from the newspaper. Her picture had been cut away, leaving Luke's, his face almost completely demolished with black ink. Her wedding date and location had been circled and anything pertaining to Luke crossed out.

So, that's how he knew where to find her. Fran was right on that end. She just had the wrong guy.

"Hey, Patterson. Come take a picture of this, will ya?"

"Sure. There's nothing else over here."

Patterson's phone clicked three times.

"You sending those to Clark?"

"You know it."

"Have him make contact with the local department and catch them up to speed." The left corner of his lips twitched upward. "Also, let them know when we're through with the Adams' case, they may want to pay a friendly visit to our buddy O'Brien."

Finding nothing else of use, Terrence pushed the power button on the computer. This guy could have left a trail leading to where he'd taken Julie on it.

Patterson stood over him as he clicked through the internet history. Adams had been to Julie's Facebook page regularly in the past month. They hadn't found a page under his name. His computer showed an account under the name Pat Murdoch.

His history also showed he'd searched the white pages and found her name on some Colonial Williamsburg sites. "Text Clark and have him get the locals to procure a search warrant. We're going to need all this stuff plus his computer."

Terrence faintly registered the tapping of a text message being typed out on Patterson's phone. He dug deeper through the web history but didn't find a single link to a map site. Did that mean he knew where he was going? Didn't need directions? Frustrated, he closed the window and shut the computer down.

"No hint at where he might be?"

"No. I'm guessing it's somewhere he's familiar with, but it couldn't be something in the family. He doesn't have family."

Patterson looked around the room. "There's nothing in here. What now?"

He motioned toward the bedroom door. "We could ask O'Brien out there, but it's doubtful he could remember anything even if Adams had bothered to say something."

"Other friends? The garage he works at?"

Terrence tapped his pen on his notebook. "Maybe." He glanced at the clock on the dresser. "Too late to go to the garage. That'll have to wait until morning. Let's ask glazed-eyes out there if he knows of any other friends. Then we'll decide whether we grab dinner on the run or sit down to eat and review our findings." He stood and put on a carefree air before stepping back into the trashed living room where a crude sitcom blared from the television.

SEVENTEEN

Terrence stabbed another bite of slightly pink steak and savored the flavor. Perry O'Brien couldn't come up with one person Todd Adams hung out with who had a last name. John, Marty, Copey, and Ian wouldn't get them far without last names. He eyed the loaded baked potato, wondering if it had cooled enough to dig into without burning the roof of his mouth. He chanced it. The flavors of potato, chives, sour cream, and bacon exploded on his tongue.

He needed to get out more. Of course, his mom was a fantastic cook. What he really needed was to get over to her place more often. But then he'd have to hear about church. He forked another bite. Eating her home cooked food might be worth it. Anything would be better than fast food or heating up whatever he happened to have in the fridge as he did most nights after a long day of work.

Patterson broke through his thoughts. "We've got the right guy this time. He's been tracking Mrs. Montgomery and researching her life."

He shoved another bite of steak into his mouth. "Yes. But that hasn't gotten us what we need."

"The guy has no family, no connection to any foster family, and friends with no last names. The worst type of suspect. No real attachments to anyone."

"Except Julie Montgomery." Terrence tapped his fork on his plate. "The thing that bothers me most is he paid January's rent already. He's not planning to come back. So what does he do with Julie? Surely, he doesn't think he'll convince her to stay with him."

Patterson looked at him over his glass of iced tea. "You know abusers."

"What's mine is mine." A knot twisted in Terrence's stomach. "Julie Montgomery doesn't stand a chance. We have to find her."

"What about her mom? She didn't seem to suspect the ex-boyfriend, but maybe if we talk to her, she'll be able to remember something." Patterson drummed his fingers on the table.

"We can always ask." He needed to call Ms. Fran anyway. She must be frantic. He chewed another bite, although the flavors had gone dull. He should call his mom, too. Check in. Tell her he loved her. He didn't do that enough. "I'll call her when we get back to the hotel."

Once back at their room, Terrence shed his coat and threw it onto the chair in the corner. Adrenaline gone, weariness spread through his body. How much sleep had he gotten the night before? Three hours, he guessed. He'd hoped to have completed this case before the end of the day and have Julie Montgomery returned safely home. Nothing about this case was going the way he planned. He strode over to his suitcase and pulled out his workout clothes. "I'm heading to the gym."

"Thought you were going to call Julie's mom."

"Gonna process first," Terrence hollered from behind the closed bathroom door. He changed and headed to the hotel fitness center.

Fifteen minutes later, he used a rag to wipe the sweat off his brow. Tucking the rag into his waistband, he lay back down and hefted the heavily weighted bar until his biceps screamed for mercy. After three repetitions of twenty, he moved to squats. His mother would throw a fit if she knew he was working out without a spotter. And while frustrated. *You make mistakes when you're emotional.*

He was making a mistake with this case. He'd done something he'd never done before. He'd allowed himself to get sucked in. The fact that Ms. Fran reminded him so much of his own mother was a viable reason. Or possibly it was due to the genuineness he saw in these people, which was such a far cry from what he usually dealt with in his line of work.

He hoisted the weighted bar back onto its home and wiped his brow again. He walked over to the water cooler and gulped down three cups of water. He dreaded calling Ms. Fran, being able to guess at her reaction when he revealed the truth about Todd Adams. Luke Montgomery would be shattered.

He crushed the cup and tossed it in the trashcan. He didn't understand why people kept secrets.

Julie had been the victim, but still, keeping her past secrets had put her in danger and would jeopardize her current relationships. "Ha."

He caught his reflection in part of the mirror that covered the entirety of one wall in the miniscule exercise room. *You won't even let yourself get into a relationship to risk ruining.*

The picture of a young woman with jet-black hair and pale, freckled skin popped into his mind. Maggie. He'd only met her briefly during his second interview at Julie Montgomery's work site, but her sad smile had captivated him. Too busy working the case, he wouldn't let himself contemplate the way his heart had raced at the touch of her tiny hand in his. He was always too busy working to consider dating. His reflection stared back at him. "I know. Dwelling on it won't do any good. Why would a nice girl like Maggie have any interest in a man like me?" He wiped his brow one more time and tossed the rag into the laundry bin.

Back to reality. Time to call Ms. Fran.

"Anything new?" he asked Patterson as the hotel room door closed behind him.

Patterson looked up from his spot on the bed, laptop open, papers strewn around him. "Nope. Nothing. Clark's traced both Julie Montgomery's cell phone and Todd Adams'. Her last ping was off a tower close to CW at six forty-two Tuesday morning. His last ping was a tower here in Lynchburg around eight o'clock Monday night."

Terrence plucked some clean sweats out of his

suitcase. "He must have gone to Williamsburg that night. Any hits on his credit card?"

"The last two charges made were at McDonald's and a gas station here in town, also around eight."

"Smart guy. Turns off his cell and uses cash."

Patterson shook his head. "Yeah. Stinks for us."

"And for Julie Montgomery." Terrence glanced at his laptop, sitting on the table in the corner. Getting back to work could wait a few more minutes. "I'm gonna hit the shower. Then I'll make the call."

Muscles aching but refreshed from the exertion and shower, Terrence emerged from the steamy bathroom determined to treat the call to Ms. Fran like any other investigation inquiry.

"Hello?" Her anticipation came thick through the line.

"Hi, Ms. Fran. It's Officer Cooper."

"Terrence, have you found anything? Do you know where my Julie is?"

Resolve melted. "We have a lead, but we still don't know where she is." He exhaled. "Ms. Fran, is someone with you?"

"Yes, Luke's here. And the Teeters."

Sue and Mark Teeter. "OK, good. I need to ask you some questions."

"You said you have a lead."

"We do. We've found out some things about Julie's ex-boyfriend, Todd Adams."

"Todd...I–"

She paused and background voices came through the line. "Sit down, Ms. Fran." "I'll get her some water."

Terrence pushed on. "Ms. Fran, are you OK?"

"Yes, I just didn't expect to hear his name. Julie hasn't mentioned him since we moved from Lynchburg."

The poor woman surely wouldn't be able to take any more blows. He wanted to make sure the next one wasn't that they'd let something happen to her daughter. "We've talked to several of Julie's friends from high school and college. Like you said before, Julie kept things to herself. Apparently, she kept things about her relationship with Adams pretty tight."

"He didn't...." She paused before continuing. "Did he hurt her? She should have known better. She wouldn't have stayed." Her last words came as a whisper.

Terrence plopped onto the bed, and the corner gave under his weight. He needed to soften the blow as much as possible. "Do you remember Julie's friend, Darla Compton?"

"Yes."

"Miss Compton is one of the friends we interviewed. She said Julie never talked much about Todd, but that one day she walked into the bathroom right after Julie got out of the shower and saw bruises."

Ms. Fran gasped. "No. She would have told me. She wouldn't have kept that from me."

Terrence leaned forward and rested his elbows on his knees. He hated breaking this woman's heart. Again. "We've dug into Adams' past. He was a foster kid taken from a violent home. He has a record."

"Oh, no." She choked back a sob. "I don't understand. Why would she put up with that? She knew better. How could I not have known or even suspected?"

"I don't know any more details about Julie's relationship with Adams, Ms. Fran. But we're pretty sure he's the reason she left Lynchburg."

"I-oh."

"Was it Julie who pushed for the move?"

"I never thought about it, but yes, she did. She looked for a job for months but didn't apply to even one in Lynchburg. I figured she simply wanted a change. Wanted to live somewhere else. When I asked her about Todd, she said she'd decided they needed to part ways. I never thought…"

He stood and strode over to the table with his computer and all his notes. "She never gave you any reason to think anything different. Like you said, Julie let people know what she wanted them to know."

"True. But this. She knew I'd left. Why would she stay so long?"

"We don't know when the relationship went sour." Although his calculations told him at least three years before the move. "She followed your example, though. She left. I'm sure you empowered her to get out of what had become a harmful relationship. There's no way to have all the answers until we get Julie back. And to do that, I need to ask you some more questions."

Ms. Fran's breath shuddered. "OK."

"Did Julie ever go away with Todd?"

"No, not alone. A couple of times she went to the beach or skiing with some friends and he went along, but that was early on. I don't think they ever took a trip alone together."

"OK. How about Todd by himself? Did Julie ever talk about Todd going hunting?"

"No, I don't think so. She didn't talk about him a lot. I can't remember."

Terrence had been optimistic about Ms. Fran holding the key to where Adams had taken Julie. That the one piece of information they needed to find her might lay with her mother. Now his hopes were dashed. If she had something helpful, it might help Ms. Fran feel less guilty. She had nothing to feel guilty about, but somehow, he knew she did. "Don't worry. That she would have said anything to you about somewhere he might have gone was a long shot. We'll turn something up here."

"I'm so sorry. I wish I could be more helpful. I wish I'd have known."

"I'd wager Julie didn't want you to know. And you have been helpful."

"Yeah. My secretive Julie." Ms. Fran paused. "Did you say here? You're in Lynchburg?"

"We are."

"But Todd's not there? You're sure he took Julie?"

Terrence glanced at the closed file. He debated how much to tell her. He'd asked a lot of her. The least he could do was give her the bare bones of what he'd found. "He's not here. He told his roommate he was going on vacation. His absence could be a coincidence, but..."

"You don't think so."

Sighing, he decided against trying to fully protect Ms. Fran. "No. What we've found so far is pretty clear. Todd seems to be the guy we're looking for."

"I'll do what I can then. I'll search Julie's things from Lynchburg. We still have several boxes in the attic she never unpacked. If I find anything, I'll let you know."

His shoulders relaxed. The determination had returned to Ms. Fran's voice. "You do that. There's nothing else for us to do tonight but get some rest and start fresh in the morning. Hopefully, Julie will be home this time tomorrow."

"I'll be praying she will be. Thank you, Terrence."

"You're welcome."

He hung up, plugged his phone into its charger, and turned to face Patterson.

"How'd it go?"

"As well as expected. She had no idea about the abuse."

Patterson shook his head as he pushed off his bed and strolled to the bathroom. "What a tragedy." He stopped at the door and glanced back at Terrence. "So we get a good night's sleep and go to the garage first thing?"

"Yep." The bathroom door clicked shut.

~*~

Fran hung up the phone and refused to meet

Luke's gaze. He sat next to her, holding her free hand, legs bouncing anxiously. She'd kept her eyes focused downward since Terrence mentioned Todd Adams and the things they had found. The officer's vagueness when referring to the evidence caused her to think the worst.

She should have known that Julie had been in an abusive relationship. She knew all the signs and had recognized them instantly in others, even helped a friend in Lynchburg get to the women's shelter with her two small children. Closing her eyes, she blocked out the present and searched for a clue. She'd never seen a bruise on Julie.

Thinking back, Julie had worn long sleeves a lot. Even in moderate temperatures. Never sunglasses inside, though. Maybe he'd been smart enough to stay away from her face. Unlike Stuart. Her ex-husband had never been that bright.

Violent and smart. Not a good combination. Especially if he had Julie. After speaking to Terrence, she assumed Todd was their only suspect. *Oh, God. Protect my baby.*

She should have protected her babies earlier. Gotten them out and away from that life in time to prevent this. And Rebecca. Her heart ached anew at the knowledge her eldest daughter had not fared well after leaving home. Both her girls now living nightmares, because she hadn't been strong enough.

Hands shook her shoulders, and she opened her eyes.

"Fran." Luke stared at her. "Fran, what was that

all about? Who's Todd?"

"Todd Adams. Julie dated him for a while."

Looking like he'd been punched, Luke sat back. "The guy from Lynchburg? But why? Why now?"

"I...I don't know." The image from the sketch artist's drawing appeared in Fran's mind. Was it Todd? A lot of time had passed since she'd seen him. The guy in the picture hadn't left much of his face to be seen. But yes, in the depth of her soul, the picture matched up.

She should've seen it sooner. Julie'd been missing three days. She could've helped out more by thinking harder, better scrutinizing the picture. She just never thought–

"Ms. Fran." Sue's soft, soothing voice broke through Fran's inner dialogue. She turned her gaze at the concerned face. When had Sue moved to the floor, kneeling in front of her?

"Has Officer Cooper found something?"

"Yes, um..." She played with the strings on her apron. "They talked to some of Julie's school friends. One of them..." She looked at Luke. "I didn't know either. She didn't tell me either." Hot tears burned their way down her cheeks.

Luke's hand, moments before tenderly encompassing her small one, stiffened into a fist beside hers. Misery filled his eyes and contorted his face. "What...didn't she...tell you?" He spoke deliberately.

"The friend, she said she saw bruises on Julie one time when they were in college."

A guttural cry escaped Luke's lips. "No."

Fran's wringing, shaking hands reached for his. "I didn't know. She never acted—there was nothing that would've given it away. I, of all people, would have seen it." A sob broke through and wracked her shoulders. Sue's comforting arms wrapped around her. "Why didn't I see it?" she murmured.

Luke pulled away and shot off the couch. "I can't take this. Not more secrets. Not more—" He choked on his words. "How bad is it, Fran?"

"They found where he lives, but he's not there. They're trying to find out where he went."

"That's not what I meant. What did they find on this guy?" Every word burst with emotion.

"Nothing good." Fran crumbled under his aching gaze and the burden of what Officer Cooper had told her.

Faintly, over the din of her own tears, she heard Luke's strained voice. "I gotta get out of here."

He turned and strode to the front door. He slammed it shut a moment later, and she jumped. Mark met her gaze then headed out as well. Her tears slowed and the convulsing sobs lessened.

Sue's soothing voice broke through again. "Fran, honey, you're not alone."

One more body shaking breath and Fran wiped away the last few tears. She took a deep breath. "I know. Thank you for being here. This is all so much."

"No, Fran." Sue lifted her chin. "I'm glad to be here. We all love Julie and Luke. And we love you. But that's not what I mean."

Fran cocked her head to the side, scrunching her

brows in confusion.

"How many times when Hunter was in the neonatal unit did you remind me that he was in God's hands? When I thought I'd never hold my baby, never see him smile or take a first step, how many times did you tell me God was with me, heart aching with mine? Only He knew the outcome. Your words, Fran. Words of truth."

Another shaking sigh let out the stress and guilt and anguish. "I said that?"

"You did. They were hard words when I had no answers, when the doctors gave us almost no hope. But they were true. God was with us, and He is with you. Let Him carry this. Yell, scream, throw a fit, and know He can take it."

Fran forced a weary smile. "I have." Tears filled her eyes once again. "Now I want to yell at Julie."

Sue met her challenging gaze with understanding. "OK. Yell at her."

Fran snorted then hiccupped. A lone tear traveled down her cheek and dripped off her chin. "I just want her back."

"We all do."

Sue's face held no accusation or blame. Only love and shared heartache.

"You haven't even asked," Fran said.

"I don't need to know."

"My husband was abusive. He hurt Julie. We left and started a new life. I never thought she'd allow it to happen to her again."

Sue's hand rubbed Fran's shoulder and arm. "We

don't know everything."

"Enough. Officer Cooper said Todd has a violent history. I couldn't tell Luke that."

Sue laid her forehead against Fran's temple. "We can't change anything that's already happened. We can stand at God's door and pound on it until He brings Julie home safely."

"Yes, we can."

"Father, we come to You confused, angry, scared. We don't know why this has happened to Julie, and we want her back home. Take care of her, Lord. Nothing is impossible with You. We praise You for the love and mercy You show us every day. Overflow that love today, on us and on Julie. Keep her safe. Let her know You are with her."

The dampness from Sue's tears seeped through Fran's hair. She reached up and held her hand.

"Don't let us drown in our grief and confusion. Bring our focus back to You, to Your greatness, Lord. We pour our tears into Your hands."

Sue wrapped her arms around Fran and held her, as she gripped the words her friend offered up for them all.

~*~

Luke paced back and forth in front of his truck. "How much more can I take? Secrets on top of secrets. I feel like I don't know my own wife." Rage fueled Luke's words and his feet. Underneath, though, a stronger emotion threatened to erupt. Fear gripped his heart. "My Julie. My beautiful Julie spent how much of her life taking abuse. And now—now what?"

Out of the corner of his eye, he saw Mark leaning against the back of Fran's car. He waited for the rebuke, for Mark to tell him he had lost it, that he should be focusing on finding Julie, not being mad at her. The reprimand didn't come.

Stopping, he turned to his friend. "Why did she keep so much from me? Why didn't I know?"

Mark's hands raised and he shrugged his shoulders. "I don't know."

"If I'd have known, I could've protected her. Watched out for her better."

Mark kicked away from the car and shoved his hands in his pockets. "What would you have done? Followed her around everywhere? Never let her out of your sight?"

Luke ran his hands down his face. "Maybe. I don't know. But if she had told me, I could've done something."

"This isn't your fault, man."

"I should've known."

Mark stepped closer. "You didn't. You can't change that. Being mad at Julie and being mad at yourself doesn't change anything."

Luke glared at Mark. "What do you know? You have your perfect marriage with your perfect wife and your perfect child with another on the way. I bet Sue never kept the tiniest secret from you."

Mark lost all appearance of nonchalance as he moved closer. His face hardened. "Perfect. Have you forgotten? I was the one driving when we were in the accident that sent Sue into preterm labor. I'm the one she didn't talk to for almost two months while our son held onto life by a thread. No, neither Sue nor I are perfect, but we never gave up. On each other. Or on God."

Luke's resolve crumbled, and he choked through threatening tears. "No. I know everything's not perfect. All this information is just so overwhelming." Swallowing the golf-ball sized lump now in his throat, he struggled as the earth-shaking fear broke through. "What can I do? My wife's missing, and the only thing I can do is stand here and learn about more secrets she kept from me. I couldn't stop this, and I can't fix it." He collapsed back against the front of his truck, letting the bumper hold him up.

Mark dropped beside him. "I get it. The helplessness. When the one you love the most needs you the most and you can't get to her."

Luke lost the battle with the tears he'd been fighting. "I don't know what to do. How do I get through the night? How do I wake up tomorrow and go through another day without Julie?" He ran his hands over his face. "What do I do?"

"You get angry. You feel the fear. Then you get on your knees."

Luke balled his fists.

"Have you ever felt this desperate about anything before in your life? Ever needed God's all-knowing, all-loving presence more?"

Rolling the question through his mind, Luke

thought back to his father in the hospital, kept alive by machines after his heart attack. He had desperately wanted his dad to make it. They had doctors giving them information, though. They had time to talk to his dad, even if he couldn't talk back. They had time to say good-bye. Even then, he hadn't felt this despondent. "No."

"Then get on your knees, man. Pray every thought you have to God and let Him take it. Know if you go to bed tonight and wake up tomorrow without Julie, you won't be waking up without God."

Luke shook his head. "But that won't bring her back. What will I do if she doesn't come back?"

"Prayer may not bring her back. But it will get you through today. Tomorrow. We had no guarantees Hunter would make it out of the hospital to go home with us. We clung to God, and Hunter came home. God doesn't promise us everything will always go our way, but He does promise nothing will separate us from His love. Hold on to that. Just for today."

"Like it's that simple," he scoffed.

"I didn't say it was simple. But it's the best thing to do." Mark clapped Luke on the shoulder. "I bet those ladies in there are praying. Let's go join them."

Luke shoved himself off the bumper. He couldn't do anything else to help Julie. He might as well pray.

EIGHTEEN

Exhaustion pulled at Terrence from every angle, but his mind refused to be still. He'd gone to bed an hour before, but sleep eluded him.

Hunting. He'd told his roommate he was going hunting. He could be anywhere, tucked into a house, cabin, or obscure resort. He could be thirty minutes away, three hours away, or half a day away.

Adams would have to be somewhere he could pay cash and didn't have to use an I.D. Surely, he would've planned for the event knowing they'd suspect him. He'd planned everything else so carefully. Did he rent a place from someone he knew? Or borrowed the cabin of a friend or acquaintance without them knowing? If he knew no one would be there, he could have simply taken it upon himself to confiscate a place for his use. From what Terrence had learned, he didn't doubt Adams would take whatever he wanted without mentioning a word to anyone.

He could be impossible to find.

He rolled onto his side, trying to block the light

shining from the vanity area. Every file, every paragraph, every picture filtered through his mind. He didn't want to miss even the minutest detail.

Patterson shuffled out of the bathroom and plopped onto his bed. Moments later the buzz of his snores reverberated throughout the room.

Terrence flung himself off the bed. Pacing the floor, he continued to sort and file the copious amounts of information in his mind's folders. The battery icon on his cell phone blinked as it charged. He groaned. He hadn't called his mom. The digital display read ten thirty-five. She'd probably be in bed reading. Snatching up the phone and unplugging it, he slinked out the door and down the hallway to the stairwell.

"Hey, handsome." The familiar voice and greeting pushed a smile past his tension.

"Hey, Ma. You weren't asleep were you?"

"No, hon. Just reading. How's the case?"

"Going. I'm not home yet."

"But you have a lead?"

"Yes, we have a—" There was no way she could know that. She had to be guessing, or... "Who've you been talking to, Ma?"

"Talking to?"

His smile returned. She couldn't fool him. He knew her too well and was good at his job. "Yes. You sound like you already know we have a lead, not like you're wondering."

His mother snickered. "OK. You got me. I talked to Fran."

Rolling his eyes, he found it hard to be annoyed.

"So you've resorted to checking up on me through the family involved in my case?"

"I wasn't checking up on you. I like Fran. She's a lovely woman and going through a really tough time right now. I thought she could use some extra support and prayer."

He sat, resting his elbows on his knees and chin on his free palm. "I'm sure she appreciates it."

"And you have some information, but you've hit another dead end."

How did his mom figure out so much? Terrence never said those words to Ms. Fran. "No, not a dead end. Just have to wait until tomorrow to interview more people."

"Son?"

Terrence recognized this voice and braced himself.

"Have you prayed about this case? About getting the right leads and finding Julie Montgomery?"

"Prayers don't solve cases, Ma. Evidence does."

"Don't you think an all-knowing God can put evidence into your hands?"

If God was all-knowing, why didn't he stop Todd Adams? "Yes, Ma."

"Then pray about it. Fran and Luke along with all their friends are. So am I."

He stood and pushed his doubts away. He didn't need religion distracting him from the case. "I'll think about it, Ma. I love you. I'm going to get some sleep now."

Back in the hotel room, he tucked in under the thin sheet and quilt. He fell asleep with visions of damaged pictures, bloody hands, and praying faces swirling together in his mind.

~*~

Fran rested her head back and closed her eyes. How could she feel both weary and rejuvenated? Sue, Mark, Luke, and she had prayed for an hour. Nothing had changed since before then. They had no new information, nothing tangible to offer them hope. But hope welled inside her. Crying out to God didn't quell the fear completely, but it helped subdue her anxieties.

Luke and Julie were blessed to have friends like Mark and Sue. She was blessed to be counted as part of their circle. These young people, so much younger in years but older in faith, had such wisdom. As much as God had taught her in her few years of following Him, they taught her how much she had left to learn.

Sitting up and glancing at the idle phone, more warm thoughts flooded Fran. Marta Cooper had become a fast friend through this horrible situation. She'd called several times since their initial conversation, and while Fran suspected the calls had something to do with Marta keeping track of Terrence and the case, she also felt the genuineness of her new friend's prayers and encouragement. God certainly made His point clear. She was not alone as she struggled with Julie's disappearance.

She wasn't alone in worrying about Julie as a parent either. The phone glared at her. Fighting the urge to flee from her own thoughts, she took several deep breaths. She'd rehashed over and over the phone call from Stuart two days before. There didn't seem to be the slightest hint of the man she'd been married to. Fran compared that with what Terrence had reported from his visit with Stuart. All the new information she had about Stuart added up to true change. She sat, rooted to her bed. Her daughter most likely had been abducted by an abusive boyfriend who'd gone off the deep end. Still, she contemplated calling her former abuser. Could two lives take such divergent paths after starting out so similar?

Rebecca's beautiful sixteen-year-old face burst into her mind. Fran reached over and pulled out the picture she kept in the bottom of her bedside table drawer. She stroked the cheek of the girl with a sad-eyed smile. She hadn't gotten out in time for Rebecca. That remained her biggest regret. A vice tightened its grip on her heart. If only she'd had the courage to leave earlier. If only she had put her girls first from the beginning. If only...

The vice squeezed and anguish returned. She could continue beating herself up for every wrong decision she'd made in the past, or she could embrace and cling to the words lifted in prayer that evening.

"God, You know every word we uttered for Julie tonight. I bring my precious Rebecca to You, too. Every word, Lord. Let her know You love her. Protect her and draw her to You. Soften her heart and let her open herself to healing and forgiveness."

Praying again returned the unexplainable sense of peace she'd felt before she let her thoughts run away from her. Before she could change her mind, she picked up the phone and dialed the number still on caller I.D.

"Hello?" the distinct male voice answered.

"Hi, Stuart."

Silence crept on the line.

"Have they found Julie? Is she OK?"

She fought the lump in her throat. "The police have a lead, but they haven't found her yet. An ex-boyfriend-"

"Oh, no. Fran, I'm so sorry. Was he, did he hurt her before?"

"I didn't know. We still don't know for sure." Her shoulders slumped, and she swallowed that pesky lump again. "But it looks that way."

"What can I do? Should I come there? Can I help in any way?"

Shock kept her silent. What had she expected? Nothing. She had expected nothing. "I don't think so. There's nothing any of us can do right now but wait." And pray.

"OK. Let me know, if you can, as soon as they find her."

As soon as they find her. She breathed in the words. "I will."

"Thank you, Fran. I'll be praying."

The phone went dead then began beeping. Fran clicked it off. Stuart had said he'd be praying. That he could have changed *that* much seemed unimaginable. She'd given credence to the idea that God could work the impossible, change anyone, but she'd never considered that Stuart would find God. She shook her head. If God could do that, then He certainly could do anything. Even bring Julie home safely.

~*~

The first rays of sunlight stole through the slit left in between the heavy, dark curtains that had been drawn in the hotel room the night before. Anxious to get the day started, Terrence had been watching the clock slowly relay the time minute by minute for almost two hours. Each time the digits changed, they seemed to be screaming, "Not time yet; not time yet."

He'd sifted through the information they had gathered in the past three days like a museum curator, turning each piece of data over slowly, inspecting it at every angle. He didn't want to miss anything. He had not gotten the pieces in order. They'd been scattered about, as an art collection that had been auctioned off to pay a tremendous debt of its former owner. The masterpiece was Julie Montgomery's life, and every little item worked together collectively to lead him to her. Still, though, pieces remained missing. Today, he would hunt down those last outstanding fragments.

He hadn't overlooked anything. Of that, he'd become sure. Throwing the covers aside, he leapt out of bed and strode toward the shower. He emerged fifteen minutes later.

Patterson's gaze and the droning of newscasters on the television greeted him. Patterson nodded at him, meandered to his own suitcase, then headed to the shower.

Pacing himself as he finished the morning routine of shaving and brushing his teeth, Terrence willed the next hour and a half away. The car repair shop Todd Adams worked at didn't open until nine. That meant they wouldn't be able to question anyone until shortly before the late hour struck. The hour that would also officially signal four full days since a distressed Luke Montgomery had walked into the police station demanding help in finding his wife.

The laptop fired up quickly, and he once again opened the collection of files relating to the case. He didn't need to see the words. They had become ingrained in him down to the core of his being, but it gave him something to do as he waited. The television droned on, giving twenty second blurbs of cases other officers dealt with elsewhere, states of nations he'd never visit, the expected outcomes of the upcoming football games, and a full twelve minutes devoted to the latest and greatest gadgets to buy for Christmas and the most recently separated celebrity couple.

He pulled up the files he wanted to focus on today. The files on Todd Adams. He read again the gruesome details of the scars and evidence of the brutality Adams had lived with before being taken away from his biological parents. Kids like that always went one of two ways. They either helped others in similar situations or became what they had once abhorred. Todd Adams obviously had solid membership in the latter group.

A burst of steam puffed out when Patterson

opened the door and stepped to the vanity.

Terrence continued reading the complaints from the foster parents. Mean to the younger kids. Skips school often. Said he brought a knife to school because older kids had threatened him. He scoffed. He'd believe that when a bridge was built to Hawaii.

The details of the police report involving the bar brawl intrigued him the most. The date of the incident happened to be within two months after Julie and her mom had moved from Lynchburg to Williamsburg. Enough time for a boiling kettle to simmer over and explode. Especially when Adams could find no trace of her.

He leaned back and steepled his fingers. How long had Adams looked for her? And what lengths had he gone to?

What was it Darla Compton said? He tapped his fingers together, searching for her words.

Adams had called her after Julie moved. Terrence leaned forward and tapped and clicked his way to Julie Montgomery's social media page. She had everything set to only let friends see, but they had ways around those security measures. Had Todd Adams also gotten around them?

Julie's page filled the screen, her smiling wedding portrait gracing the top left corner. They had gone through her friends like sifting through muddy water for gold but had only glanced at her information page. Her profile didn't contain much. Her gender, her status as married, and her religious views posted as Christian. No favorite books, TV shows, or musicians.

No e-mail, phone number, or place of work. She hadn't even entered where she lived.

Terrence leaned back again. Even if Adams had weaseled his way into her life through the computer, which the quick perusal he'd made through Adams' Internet history suggested he had, he hadn't garnered any valuable details from social media. Julie Montgomery seemed intelligent. And careful. Where had she left herself vulnerable?

The joy-filled eyes answered him. She'd begun to crave normalcy. She'd fallen in love with a normal man who loved her back. She'd created a normal life–with friends and family and a job she enjoyed. Normal people put their wedding announcement in the paper when they got married. That desire for normal, the culmination of everything Julie Montgomery had worked diligently to control in her life, caused the rest to crumble.

"You ready?" Patterson's voice broke through his reverie.

"Yeah." He closed the stacked windows and shut down the laptop. Pushing the chair back, he stood. "Been ready for hours.

Patterson gestured toward the clock. "Only a few minutes after eight. Grab something to eat from the lobby before we head out?"

Terrence grabbed his coat and slipped it on. "Yeah."

Forty minutes later, he steered the car onto the small concrete parking lot in front of Mike's Garage. The humble brick building spanned the small lot, leaving only a dozen parking spaces out of the way of the two large garage doors.

Sounds of an impact wrench floated through the open doors. The odors of oil, grime, and hand cleaner assailed his nostrils as they walked across the small parking lot. He pulled the white door littered with product stickers open and entered the dimly lit room. Light from the early morning sun filtrated in from the two large windows on either side of the door, but it didn't quite make up for the half-lit florescent lights in the ceiling. A young guy in a blue jump suit stood behind the dingy counter. The tall, skinny boy with sandy blond hair's nametag read, Pete.

"Can I help ya?"

Flashing his badge and forcing a grin, Terrence answered. "Yes. We're looking for Todd Adams. We have a few questions for him."

"Aww. Todd ain't here. He took off huntin'. Ain't taken off more than a day or two since he's been here. Then all of a sudden, he hits the road for two weeks. Boss ain't happy, but Todd's a good mechanic."

He glanced over at Patterson. "You happen to know where he's hunting?"

Pete plopped on a round stool and leaned on the counter. He subconsciously picked at the grit under his fingernails. "Naw. Can't see how a guy can hunt fer two weeks." He shook his head. "Bet he's got a girl he's gone off with. That's what I'd do." He looked up from his fingernails and gave a lopsided grin.

If he only knew. "How about anyone else? Anybody here Todd's close to and might know where he went?"

"Um, Bubba, I guess. They work a lot of jobs together."

"Is Bubba here today?"

"Yup. In there workin' already. A radiator, I think."

"Great. Think we could borrow Bubba for a few minutes?" Terrence leaned down and met the teenager eye to eye. "We won't keep him long. I promise." With any luck, Bubba would have what they needed and they'd be on their way to find Adams and Julie Montgomery within minutes.

"Shuwa. I'll get 'im." The boy popped off the stool and pushed his way through the door leading to the garage. Muffled voices leaked through the door. Metal clanged on concrete. The door pushed open. Behind the rail thin Pete followed a slightly shorter, muscled man with dark crewcut hair. The scowl on his face gave evidence that he didn't like being pulled from a job. The blue jumpsuit he wore was an exact duplicate of Pete's, except his nametag read, Bubba.

Bubba stood behind the counter and crossed his arms. "What do you want?"

Closing and relaxing his fists, Terrence forced patience. "Good morning. We're looking for Todd Adams. Have a few questions for him and heard you might know where to find him."

Disinterest etched Bubba's face. "I might. What's it to ya?"

Terrence pulled his notebook and pen out of his coat pocket. "I told you. We have some questions to ask him. That's all."

"He's on vacation. Ask him when he gets back." Bubba spun toward the door.

Reaching across the counter with his left hand, Terrence grabbed Bubba's shirt front, stopping his forward momentum. He pulled the mechanic close, forcing his arms to unfold and get caught between his body and the counter.

Within inches of the man's face, Bubba's hot breath huffed fast.

"You listen to me. These questions are part of an investigation into a missing woman. You will tell us what you know, or we will gladly haul your arrogant butt down to the station. Your choice. Give us an answer now, or do it downtown while charges for obstruction of justice and aiding a kidnapping are filed."

Terrence recognized the fight in the man's eyes. Could feel the tenseness in his muscles underneath the grasped shirt. His gaze didn't waver. Precious moments ticked away.

"Fine," Bubba spat.

Terrence let go of the man's shirt but still held his gaze. "Great. Now, let's try again. Where is Todd Adams?"

Bubba flattened out the wrinkles in his shirt. "We got a family cabin in New Kent County. The place is perfect for huntin' so I told Todd he could have it for a couple weeks."

"What's the address?" His pen moved along the small lined paper.

"I don't know."

He swallowed the desire to punch the cocky mechanic. "I thought we covered your lack of knowledge already."

Lifting his hands in defense, Bubba shrugged his shoulders. "I really don't know. I just know how to get there. Gave Todd directions."

"OK. Let's start with who owns the cabin. Then you give me those directions."

"The cabin belongs to my uncle, Robert Caughman."

He scribbled the name and then the directions. Good grief. He was in the middle of nowhere. But at least the location was close to home.

Flipping his notebook shut, Terrence slid the pen in the spiral and tucked them safely into his inner coat pocket. "Thanks."

Bubba scowled and stormed out.

Pete stood wide-eyed and tongue-tied.

Terrence nodded at the young mechanic. "Thank you."

Pete shook off his stupor. "Did Todd really kidnap some girl?"

"Looks that way. Now we'll be able to find out for sure."

Back in the car, he fought the urge to head straight back toward home and instead steered the car through the traffic back to the hotel.

"Thanks for not interfering."

Patterson chuckled. "I would have, but the guy deserved it. Plus, you stepped over no line that I saw."

He glanced at his passenger. Working with a partner regularly wouldn't be so bad if it was someone as sensible as Patterson. "Well, thanks anyway."

He'd run over the scenarios countless times. Now he replayed every possibility and strategy in his mind, having a clearer picture of the landscape they'd be dealing with. The cabin Bubba had described sat in the middle of nowhere. Isolated from other houses, down a long gravel lane. Surrounded by acres and acres of woods. Adams would have plenty of time to spot them. The element of surprise would not be on their side.

They'd have to come up with a way to make it so. They needed to scope out that cabin, find out where he held Julie Montgomery, how secure he had things. Would they be able to signal her that they were there? Somchow get her to hide and protect herself. Todd Adams wouldn't be happy to be found.

Finding Julie had been the initial problem. The one Terrence now faced felt greater. He needed a way to get her out of the clutches of Todd Adams without endangering her life.

Back at the hotel, Terrence and Patterson stuffed their personal belongings into open suitcases. Having zipped his shut, Terrence gathered his case file, laptop, and other work materials and stuffed them into his black laptop case.

"Call Clark. Have him contact New Kent's department. Tell him to forward all the files we have on Adams and give them the essentials of the case." He closed the bag and perused the room to make sure he left nothing behind.

Patterson finished packing and flung all the towels on the floor outside the bathroom. He pulled his phone out.

"Tell them we need a negotiator and sniper, so we'll need to get the state in on this, too." Terrence glanced at the clock adorning the table between the two double beds. "We'll be there around noon."

Patterson nodded, dialed his phone, picked up his suitcase, and followed Terrence out the door. Terrence sorted through the new information again as they waited for the elevator, peripherally listening as Patterson relayed his message back to the office. They parted ways on the first floor. Terrence turned in the room keys and met Patterson by the car.

"Done. They'll have everyone gathered by the time we get there. Clark's coming ,too, since he dug up most of the info."

He tossed his bags in the trunk, allowed Patterson to do the same, and slammed it. Sliding into his seat, he cranked the engine. The ride was going to be long. Four days had passed since Luke Montgomery reported his wife missing. Three more hours would pass before the team who'd design and carry out her rescue got together. He hoped Julie Montgomery could afford those extra three hours. He also wished he had the confidence in prayer that his mother had. The drive home would be perfect for such belief. But Julie Montgomery's fate was held in the hands of men. The man who had abducted her and the men who'd try to save her.

NINETEEN

Julie fought the nausea by taking slow, deep breaths. The bowl of oatmeal she'd eaten earlier that morning threatened revolt. She wanted to pray. Tried to pray but couldn't put more than two words together. Please, Lord.

She needed strength. She needed to feel good. She needed to be able to think.

My power is made perfect in weakness.

Sliding down the bed, Julie drooped with weariness. She'd never known such weakness before. Weakness in the face of terror, yes. Feeble and helpless against brutality, yes. But she didn't understand being so languid that sitting up in bed drained her.

Her friends had talked about the halting impact pregnancy had on them. Only months before, Sue complained daily about feeling like she never spent time with Hunter because she fell asleep almost immediately after getting home from work every day. Her pregnancy would explain the sudden depletion of all her energy.

My power is made perfect in weakness.

No. Julie's fatigue came from more than just the pregnancy. Closing her eyes against the ever-present reminder of where she was, she continued breathing slowly. The smell of wood burning didn't help settle her stomach.

She breathed in power with the faint aroma of smoke. She exhaled weakness. And fear. That was the other element pulling on her, sapping any energy she might have had left. God was with her. She'd reminded herself hundreds of times in the last few days. Still, the words to stay strong, to let go of the fear, hadn't penetrated to the depths of her soul.

The memories that assailed her every time she saw Todd's face froze her mind and her prayers. The terror once again crept out of its hiding place and smashed any resolve she'd built up in the quiet moments. As of yet, he hadn't hit her. The threat of it, the recollection of the pain that accompanied his fury proved enough to immobilize her.

Oh, Lord. Help me.

This time, the contents of her stomach halted her prayers. She needed to get to the bathroom. Now.

Mustering up all the voice she could, she called his name.

Arrogant smile pasted on his face, he waltzed over and leaned on the doorframe. "You rang?"

"I need to go to the bathroom."

He pushed off the molding and narrowed his eyes. "What's wrong?"

She pushed herself up and flung her legs over the

bed. Breathe. Focus on breathing. "Now, please."

Todd rushed over and hurriedly loosed the complex knot.

Holding her hand over her mouth as she rushed across the small room, she didn't have time to close the door before she fell in front of the toilet and emptied the contents of her stomach into it. She heaved until her stomach spasms quit then collapsed on the cold linoleum floor. After a couple moments, she pushed herself up and flushed the toilet. The weariness still pulled at every muscle, but at least she no longer had the nausea to deal with. She stood, washed her hands, and rinsed her mouth out with the cold, refreshing water. Shuffling back to the bed and sitting down, she had only the slightest moment to enjoy feeling better before Todd darkened the open doorway.

Her stomach twisted but not with queasiness. With the ever-present fear. Everything came to a screeching halt, including her praise to God for reprieve from the nausea and enjoying feeling halfway normal for a few minutes. Instead, she focused on nothing but the fury on his face.

He was mad. At least she hadn't thrown up on him. Her heart pumped blood through her veins as if to make up for the sluggishness of her brain and every other muscle in her body. With each beat coursed dread. The last two times she'd seen that look, he'd stormed out of the room. Every other time, he'd let the storm loose on her. Now the dark clouds brewed in his eyes. He folded his arms.

"What was that?"

"I got sick. I must have a bug or something." The trembling worked its way from her belly to the far reaches of her fingertips.

"You got sick yesterday, too."

"Yes."

Two steps and he'd covered the distance between the door and the end of the bed. "Bugs don't work that way. A little sick here, a little sick there."

She offered a weak shrug. "I don't know. All viruses are different."

"You're making yourself sick," he thundered.

"What?"

He took one more step and stood beside her resting spot on the bed, his face red. "You know I can't stand that stuff. Sickness and stench." He grabbed her by each arm and jerked her up. "You're doing it on purpose."

She resisted the urge to get a hand up high enough to wipe his spit off her cheek. The pain of strong fingers digging into her flesh stole the last of any peace she'd held onto moments before. She struggled to speak. "I'm not. I promise."

"There's no other explanation. If you were truly sick, you'd be sick and get it over with. You're trying to keep me away."

Shaking her head was the only response she could muster.

"Don't lie to me." Todd flung her back on the bed and pinned her below the weight of his body. His knees dug into her thighs as he cuffed her wrists together with one of his hands. He grabbed a handful of hair with his free hand and yanked.

She yelped.

"You are mine. Get used to it. Nothing will change my mind."

You were bought with a price. The words quelled Julie's fears.

I am not his. I am Yours.

A blow to her ribs popped Julie's eyes open. She struggled to breath, but the fear did not return. "You look at me when I'm talking to you."

Calmness looked into fury. *I am Yours, Lord. You are with me always.*

Todd stared. But she didn't let out a peep. A headache began growing from her sore scalp. Pain radiated in her thighs. Her left side ached. Yet she held her gaze steady.

Thank You, Lord. Thank You that I'm not alone this time.

The grip on her wrists tightened. "What are you doing?"

"Nothing." Not even a wince when he squeezed her wrists more.

He glared, and his angry gaze searched her face. Finally, he flung her hands up and pushed his bulk away. "Whatever you're doing, it's not going to work. Hear me?"

Julie's gaze didn't waver. Had he really just stopped?

"Do you hear me?"

She whispered, more from her sore ribs than from anything else. "Yes."

"Good." He spun around and stomped out the door, slamming it behind him. This time, a key twisted in the lock.

Finally, she breathed. Heaving from facing down a giant. The deep breaths sent shards throughout her chest. Had he broken a rib? At least he'd punched her side and not her stomach. Her hands, both left free for the first time, cradled her still flat stomach. A tiny bud of a life fought to bloom there. The rest of her body didn't matter, as long as he didn't come near her baby.

Her head pounded now, but a grin played on her lips. He'd laid his hands on her. Certainly left bruises. But he hadn't gotten to her soul. She had feared his wrath more before it came than she did in the midst of it. Like Benjamin Franklin, who'd stood in the middle of a storm and harnessed the power of lightning, she felt victorious. She'd gotten struck, but she had also appropriated a power much greater. Her Lord was with her.

Stroking her stomach, she prayed for her baby's safety and thanked God for her own. Bruises would heal.

When had Todd lost his grip over her. Not in the shadow as a past threat. Not when she'd first come to know God. Not when she lay securely in the arms of Luke as his wife. Not until she stared him down and refused to give up her spirit along with her body.

What were the verses? The world can destroy the body but not the soul. Before, Julie had let Todd have her completely. Now she belonged to God. She had enough of His Word stored up in her heart to be able to hear Him through the chaos Todd incited.

Lord, I know what he's capable of. But I also know what You're capable of. Keep bringing Your word to me, reminding me of Your promises. I can't do this alone. Can't hold on all by myself. Thank You for being with me even here in the midst of a nightmare.

Julie winced as she rolled on her side and fought the nausea once again threatening. She took slow, deep breaths, exhaling the weakness within herself and inhaling the strength of the Lord she'd come to love, and now finally, to trust with every moment and detail of her life.

TWENTY

Terrence pushed through the double glass doors leading into the New Kent Sheriff's Department. He surveyed the landscape looking for a familiar face. He'd met a couple of the neighboring county's officers before. As his eyes grazed the room, he spotted the bulk of Tom Amory poking out a door to his far right. Amory met his gaze and waved him and Patterson back.

Amory was a good cop. Terrence was glad he was in on this one.

Several men sat around a metal table in the small room. He nodded at Jim Clark, who'd been heading up their research from the home office. Three other men he didn't recognize were perusing the data spread out on the table. He stifled a groan at the recognition of the sixth man. Jack Simpson, stone-faced as always, stood at the head of the table opposite the door. His piercing gaze shot up at Terrence's arrival.

"Cooper."

"Simpson."

Simpson ran his fingers through his thick, black hair. Even though the man had to be pushing sixty, he had more hair than almost all of the other men combined. Only a hint of lightening arched out from each temple. He motioned at the array of papers before the group. "Clark's caught us up on the information he sent you. I understand this character chose my district to hide out in."

After taking two long strides, Terrence grabbed the blown-up picture of Todd Adams, which was laying in the pile. He studied the picture as if it held more answers. "Yes, it looks that way."

Simpson gave a half-hearted gesture toward the man closest to him. "This is Burt Watts, state police. He's our sniper. Watts, this is Terrence Cooper, he's bringing this case from Williamsburg."

Terrence raised his eyebrows and hesitated briefly before sending a hand out. The unassuming looking man shook his hand firmly, again leaving him surprised. He'd never expected the middle-aged man with a receding hairline and dark circles under his eyes to be the sniper. Hazel eyes met his. "Cooper."

Simpson ran his fingers through his hair again as if he were waiting on children to wrap up playtime and get to business. "Sam Mattern." He motioned toward the shaved-head guy next to Watts. "He's state, too. Our negotiator."

Terrence shook the man's broad hand and nodded.

"You know Amory."

Clasping the former football player's hand,

Terrence met his gaze and nodded.

"And finally, we have Martin Heath."

Terrence eyed the kid sitting by Amory and stuck out his hand again. He raised an eyebrow at Simpson. Was this a joke?

As if to answer his unspoken question, Simpson explained. "Heath's been with us about a year. A good cop. He won't come across this type of experience easily. Good training."

Terrence glared at him. This was about saving a life, not good training.

Simpson's narrowed eyes answered back. My district. We do things my way. Try to challenge me.

Terrence worked his jaw. The case. Julie Montgomery. That's what they were there for. Not to fight over territorial issues. He broke eye contact and pulled up a chair. "Here's the deal. We know Julie Montgomery went to work four days ago but never arrived. She parked her car in her usual spot, and a witness saw her leaving shortly before seven with a guy." He shuffled some papers around. "This is the sketch we got from the witness."

Groans echoed in the room.

"I know. Not much to go on. But if you hold it up next to the picture of Adams, you can see the resemblance." Terrence demonstrated. "Same nose. Same high cheek bones."

He tossed the pictures down. "We also know that Julie Montgomery dated Adams for several years when she lived in Lynchburg, where Adams still lives. When she moved, she kept it from him until the day before she left. She broke all contact with friends there when she moved to Williamsburg and kept the details of her life with Adams secret. No one knew the relationship had been abusive except a friend who saw bruising on Julie once."

He sorted through the papers again. He pulled out Adam's police record. "In the meantime, we found this guy's record. He's not a nice guy and doesn't mind resorting to violence. If he's taken Mrs. Montgomery, which every indication shows he has, he maintains some warped idea that she's supposed to be with him."

He gazed around the room slowly, gauging the impact of the information. "That means he believes that if he can't have Julie Montgomery, no one will. He most likely won't surrender easily and has resolved to have her or kill her."

No one in the room flinched. Each seemed to understand the direness of the situation they planned to walk into.

"That's why we're all here. Otherwise..." Simpson let the rest of his statement go unspoken.

Terrence tapped his finger on the papers in front of him. "This guy means business, and so do we." His eyes darted to Mattern, meeting the man's sky blue eyes.

"You been negotiating long?"

The bald head nodded. "Eight years. Been on the force thirteen. I've done dozens of domestics."

"I'm sure you have. But how many of those domestics were planned out? Usually they're heat of the moment standoffs."

Mattern didn't waver. "True. Most are. But the animal is the same. He wants what he wants or else."

Good. He got it. Terrence inclined his head in assent and turned to Watts. He still had a hard time believing the stubbly-faced guy who wouldn't stand out in any crowd was the sniper. Kicked back in his chair with one leg propped up, Watts looked as if he were ready to go fire the remote control at a television instead of a rifle at a man's head.

"We'll need you in a prime position to protect the victim. Any hesitation and Adams may beat us to the trigger."

"No problem," he drawled. "I ain't missed a target yet. Nor 'ave I hit one too early, too late, or the wrong one."

"Good." Terrence turned to Clark. "Did we get any information on the property or cabin?"

Watts snatched a piece of paper up and laid it in front of him. "We have the basics. The property is a hundred-twenty-acre spread. There's a gravel driveway about a half mile long leading from the main road to the structure."

Terrence rolled his eyes. "So much for getting close quietly."

"That's why Heath's here." Watts dipped his head at the rookie. "His family owns property that backs up to this one. He's hunted the area his whole life. He'll get us close."

"How long will that take?"

Heath leaned forward and lifted his button nose up a notch. "There's a path a couple hundred yards from the driveway. I know it perfectly. I can get us behind the house in twenty minutes. If no one slows me down."

Terrence ignored the jibe. He figured it had been aimed more at Watts than him, anyway. The man did look like a half mile hike in the woods could do him in. "What about the house?"

Simpson plucked another sheet out and placed it next to the aerial of the property. "The best we could find were the original plans. The cabin is old, so there's only a rough sketch. There's a main room that houses the kitchen, dining, and living areas here." He pointed to the larger rectangle. "And a bedroom and bath here." This time Simpson indicated the medium and small rectangles. "That's it. About five hundred square feet."

Studying the rudimentary picture, Terrence noticed no indications of doors or windows. "What about windows? Doors?"

"I haven't been in the cabin, but I've been by it." Heath brushed a fleck of lint off his shoulder as if he were bored. "There's only one door leading in from the driveway. I'd guess it's the main room. There's one window in front and two in back."

Terrence's gut twisted at the cockiness in Heath's voice. He was certainly confident in himself. Too bad Terrence didn't share his certainty. "You're sure? You've been by the cabin how many times?"

Heath shrugged. "I don't know. My whole life. One door. Three windows. And a chimney."

Terrence steepled his fingers and processed the

new information. Their plan of attack needed to be split. They had eight guys. Only one way in.

Going up the driveway, Adams would have warning of their arrival. That might work to their advantage, if they got the sniper in place first and could get a hold on the situation. Then their arrival would focus all his attention on those coming in from the front. Terrence drummed his fingers against themselves as the gears worked.

"Cooper."

Terrence met Simpson's impatient gaze. "You gonna share with us or are we doomed to sitting here watching you think all day?"

He stilled his fingers and splayed them out flat in front of him. He checked the time. "We need all the advantage we can get. As much as I want to get this guy and get Julie Montgomery out of there after three and a half days that have surely been misery, I don't want to rush in hot-headed either." He looked at Heath. The anxiety carved on Heath's face unsettled him.

"Patterson and I haven't eaten lunch. We've been in the car for three hours and need to stretch a bit."

Simpson, Mattern, and Clark gaped at him. Simpson slammed his hand on the table. "You want us to sit on all this and wait for you to eat lunch?"

Terrence stood and rolled his stiff neck from side to side. "No. Not to wait for me to eat lunch. To wait for the right time."

"You want to enlighten us on when the right time is?"

Terrence turned toward Watts. "You tell me. What time of day is optimal for you to keep your sights on Adams and his movements without him being able to spot you?"

Watts' hazel eyes sparkled. "All things equal, it would benefit us if we went in around dusk. That'd give us more shadows to hide under in the woods and see things more clearly inside the cabin."

"Given he doesn't panic and shut the lights out," Simpson spat out.

Watts grinned. "Given that."

"OK, so we need time to survey the area, make sure no one else is around. Time for Watts to get into position." Terrence scanned the room, scrutinizing each face. Willing, ambivalent, anxious, calm, irritated, determined, prepared. Every expression as different as the men themselves. But they had all assembled in this stark room for the same purpose: to rescue Julie Montgomery and take down Todd Adams.

"Heath, you'll need to go with Watts and show him the way. Help him survey the area and pick the best spot." Terrence picked up the picture of Adams. "Clark, you know this case inside and out. Almost as much as me. You go with Watts and Heath to positively identify Adams and Mrs. Montgomery."

Clark assented with a small salute.

"The rest of us should go in two cars. Once the others are in place, we travel straight up the drive. Establish contact and begin negotiations." Terrence scrunched his brow and met Simpson' menacing stare. "Don't suppose there's a cabin phone."

"Nope."

"OK, Mattern. What do you suggest to open a line of communication?"

The bald man polished his head with a thick hand thoughtfully. "Depends how close we can get. Does he have a cell phone?"

Terrence shook his head. "Not on him. There's been no signal from it since Monday."

"That really limits our options." His head pristine and shiny, Mattern dropped his hand to the table. "We can use a bullhorn, offer him a cell phone. That's about it."

Waiting for more, Terrence played the possible scenarios over in his mind. None of them were ideal. But no one came up with any better ideas. "Fine. I guess we have no other choice." The aerial photo of the property caught his eye. "How long will it take us to get there?"

"Twenty minutes," Simpson answered.

"OK. Sunset's around quarter to six. Watts, Heath, and Clark should head up there around four. That'll give them plenty of time to get in place and feed us anything they observe. The rest of us can meet here at five."

Simpson's face flushed. "Do I have any say in this? You're in my county, you know."

Terrence held back the bitterness from his voice but spoke clearly. "This is my case. We're in your district, and I appreciate your support. And yes, you do have a say. You can say whether you join us or not." He turned from the pompous police chief to face the others. "Watts, Clark, Heath, four o'clock. Give me a call when you get in position." Terrence's hand swept in front of him. "The rest of you get some sleep, eat, do whatever you need to do to prepare. The night could prove to be a long one. I'll see you here at five."

TWENTY-ONE

Terrence arrived back at the New Kent County Sherriff's Department shortly after four-thirty. He'd rested, but the plans for the evening wouldn't let him sleep. His mind continually spun with all the possibilities. Getting Julie Montgomery out of the grasp of Todd Adams safely was their highest priority and greatest challenge. He couldn't see Adams giving up easily after so much planning. He would see Julie as his property and the officers as interfering with his business.

Catching Amory's eye, Terrence nodded. He strode by Simpson's office, pausing in the doorway.

The serious brown eyes crowned with bushy, black eyebrows looked up from the paperwork on the cluttered desk. "You're early."

He shrugged his shoulders, hiding the adrenaline already coursing through his veins. "I rested. I ate. I'm back. Clark and Heath get off OK with Watts?"

Simpson stroked his goatee. "Yep. Right at four. I suspect it'll be close to five before we hear from them."

Terrence cocked his head to the right. "I'll be in the conference room."

Simpson broke the mutual stare and returned to the files awaiting his attention. "We'll be down when I get the call."

Grateful no one else showed up early, he closed the door on the cold, stark room. He could have made the calls at home, or even in the car, but he'd put them off. Debating with himself, he'd finally concluded it was best to make the call. He didn't put much stock in prayer for himself, but his mother insisted it made a difference. If nothing else, it would make a difference to Julie Montgomery's family. Besides, he didn't want them caught completely unaware if anything went wrong tonight. Preparing for the possibility of bad news would be better than getting hit with it cold.

He debated who to call first and settled on his mom. She was the most detached from the situation. He dialed her number.

"Hello?" His mother always answered the phone like she didn't know who it was, even though she had caller I.D. The familiarity made him smile.

"Hi, Ma."

"Terrence Cooper, it's about time you checked in. I thought I'd have to file a missing report on you, too."

Sure she did. He'd gone three days without calling before. And he'd gotten the same guilt trip. "I've been busy, Ma. But we've found a strong lead in the case."

"You have? You've found Julie?"

If his mom had this much hope in her voice at hearing of the lead, he shuddered to think of how Ms.

Fran and Luke would react. "We haven't found her, exactly. We're pretty sure we know where she is and who she's with, though. The plan is to go in and get her tonight."

"That's great. Fran will be so relieved."

"We still have to get her out safely."

"Terrence, I know you can do it."

He leaned back and propped his feet on the table. "Ma, it's not that simple. We have a whole team going in. Me, a few other guys, a negotiator…and a sniper."

"A sniper?"

"The situation isn't good. We don't want it to get worse, but we have to be prepared for anything."

"I'll be praying."

He grinned. "I thought you might. And, Ma?"

"Yes, hon?"

"If you talk to Ms. Fran, don't mention the sniper. She doesn't need to worry needlessly." Or worry with good reason.

"So it's just your mother that needs to worry?"

He rolled his eyes. "You're used to being a cop's mom. Fran has enough to worry about with Julie missing. She doesn't need more to fret over."

"OK."

"So, you're going to call her?"

"I am." Her voice held determination.

"Then I'll call Mr. Montgomery." The husband would be emotional enough. Let his mom deal with Julie's mother.

After promising her he'd call immediately after they'd rescued Julie, he hung up and dialed Luke

Montgomery's number. He kicked his legs down, stood, and paced as the phone rang. He needed the right words.

"Hello?" Luke's anxious voice answered.

"Mr. Montgomery, it's Officer Cooper."

"Yes? Have you found Julie?"

Terrence glanced at the clock. Four-forty. "We have a lead. We're confident we know where she is."

A sigh of relief filtered over the line. "Finally. She's OK?"

This man so much wanted his wife back. His life back. "We haven't made contact yet. But I wanted you to know we're trying to have her home before the night's over."

"But she's OK?"

Terrence stopped pacing. He shouldn't have called. "Mr. Montgomery, we have information pointing to where she is and who has her. We'll be going in tonight to get her out."

His words met silence. The clock ticked. Terrence nodded at Patterson as he came in and closed the door behind himself.

"Mr. Montgomery?"

"Um, yes, I'm here. You said you know where she is. Where is she?"

"I can't give you that detail right now. I promise to keep you updated. Most likely, it'll be several more hours before this is resolved, but know it's almost over." At least, Terrence's part in the Montgomery's lives was almost over. Depending on how the next few hours went would determine the effect it had on their lives.

"OK. Thanks for calling. We know what to pray for now."

He hung up and the door opened again, revealing Mattern and Amory. Everyone was there except Simpson. Was he stalling or still waiting for the call from Heath?

"You ready?" Amory, the former football player, stood a few inches shorter than Terrence but had him beat in girth by more than a few inches. He had his game face on. The plan had been set, and he'd prepared.

Terrence nodded at his old comrade. He needed the veteran's steady calm. "I've been ready for this for days."

Simpson strode through the door with the rolled-up layout of the property the group had examined earlier.

"Heath, Clark, and Watts are in place. They're on a hill hidden in the woods behind the cabin." He unrolled the layout. "About here from what I can gather. They circled as much of the property as possible. Adams' vehicle is parked on the east side of the house. They're on the south side. They've seen some movement, but the windows are small. Adams is the only one they've identified. No sign of Julie yet."

Terrence leaned in. "The only direct way in is the gravel drive."

Simpson nodded.

"He'll hear us coming," Terrence voiced the obvious.

"But we already have the others in place." Simpson looked around the room. "We're all experienced here. Mattern, what do you think?"

Mattern rubbed his bald head. "He'll hear us coming and be angry, but it'll give us time to gage his reactions. With no way to see the girl at this point, we have no other option than to try to flush him out."

Terrence steepled his hands. "How will we communicate with him?"

"Bullhorn is the only way at first. We'll offer a radio."

"Guess that's all we've got," Terrence responded.

Mattern studied the map. "He picked a prime spot. I'll give him that." He turned his blue eyes toward Terrence. "I haven't lost a victim in ten years. I don't plan on today being the first."

His words were reassuring, but he also noticed what Mattern didn't say. He hadn't lost a victim, but how many negotiations had gone south causing the loss of the perpetrator? Terrence had no sympathy for Adams, but he believed in the justice of the courts.

Terrence pushed back from the table. If things got ugly, there was nothing they could do about it. Adams would choose his own fate.

"All right. Mattern, Patterson, you ride with me. Simpson, we'll follow you and Amory since you know the land better. What frequency are the others on?"

"Eighteen," Simpson answered.

Terrence nodded. "OK. Let's go."

The officers double checked their gear, Simpson rolled up the map, and they headed out.

TWENTY-TWO

Fran turned to Luke when his phone buzzed. From the look that turned from hope back to doubt, she guessed it must be Officer Cooper with an update on Julie.

The ringing of her home phone interrupted her thoughts. She desperately wanted to wait for Luke to finish his conversation and grill him, but the incessant ringing pulled her away.

"Hello?"

"Fran."

Her shoulders dropped at the now familiar voice of Marta Cooper. "Hi, Marta."

"How ya holding up?"

"OK. I think Luke's on the phone with Terrence now. From Luke's side of the conversation it sounds like something's going on."

"I know. I just got off the phone with him"

Hope surged. She focused on the picture of ten-year-old Julie on the wall. "That's good, right? He had good news?"

"He had news. They have another lead. This one has more substance to it."

Closing her eyes, she sank into a kitchen chair. "What does that mean?"

"I'm not sure exactly. Terrence seemed confident that this will be over soon though. This is what they've been working so hard at finding."

"This ordeal's not over yet but almost. My Julie's OK, and she'll be back home soon."

"Sounds that way. Why don't I come over? That way we can pray together."

Tears of gratitude for having someone to lean on filled Fran's eyes. "That'd be wonderful."

She hung up and met her son-in-law's gaze. He stood in the doorway, his face drawn down with exhaustion. "It's almost over. They've found her. Or at least found out where she is."

She patted the seat next to her. "I know. That was Marta. Terrence had called her, too. She's coming over to pray with us."

Luke sat and rested his chin on his open palms. "Somehow I think the next few hours are going to be a lot longer than the last few days."

She reached out to rest her hand on his arm. "Knowing we're so close yet can't do anything." She squeezed his arm. "But we can. We'll pray. Together."

"We need to make some more calls. Rally the troops," Luke said.

Friends. She needed them. So did Luke. The more people they had around, the less they'd watch the clock. And if anything happened…

No. She couldn't go down that path.

Fran let go of his arm and moved toward the phone. "I'll call Dawn. She should be home from work by now. Can you call Craig and Mark?"

Fran and Luke got busy making the calls. Dawn hesitated, doubtful she could find a babysitter on such short notice. Her husband, Paul, was on duty at the fire station and couldn't come or watch the kids. Fran waved at Luke, who was on the phone with Mark.

"Bring the kids." She looked at Luke as she continued speaking to Dawn. "They'll help keep our minds off things. I don't have a lot of toys, but if you bring some, we can set the kids up in the spare bedroom."

Luke relayed the same message to Mark and then to Craig when he talked to him.

She looked forward to having the kids at the house. She loved the innocence and joy they exuded. The children of Luke and Julie's friends were almost as good as having her own grandchildren but not quite.

Right now, holding onto the hope of Julie's return, God's faithfulness, and having a future with her daughter kept her from falling apart. She simply couldn't lose Julie.

Her thoughts shot to her older daughter. She now also had to do whatever it took to get Rebecca back.

Luke hung up his phone. "They'll be here within the hour."

"Good." She inhaled deeply. "I have another call I have to make." She walked toward the hallway leading to the bedrooms.

Luke's hand on her arm stopped her. "Fran?"

"I'm going to call Stuart. He needs to know."

Shock dropped Luke's jaw and widened his eyes. "Fran, you can't mean it."

"I know all this is new to you, Luke. But when Terrence found Stuart, he found a new man. From everything Terrence reported, Stuart is no longer the brutal, drunken man I married."

"But Julie, she wouldn't want him involved."

"I know. I won't give him access to her when she comes home. Luke, he already knows where she is. If he wanted to invade our lives, he could have done it a long time ago. Plus..."

His hand dropped. "Plus, what?"

"He called. After Terrence questioned him. I could hear the difference. Not in just what he said, but how he said it."

"How could you know? After one phone conversation? You said yourself he hid it well from others."

She had asked herself the same questions. "I know, Luke. I can't make sense out of it. I've been over it dozens of times in my head. I've prayed about it. The biggest factor of all, he's known where we are for years but he's let us live our lives. That in itself says a lot."

Luke frowned and shook his head.

"I know it's overwhelming. I'll keep protecting Julie if that's what she wants when she comes home." Her voice wavered. If she made it home. "But Stuart is still her father, and this may be the start to healing. For all of us." Including Rebecca.

The doorbell chimed. "Get that, will you, Luke? I'll be out in a few minutes," Fran said.

Marta's booming voice reached Fran before she closed her bedroom door.

"Hello. You must be Luke."

Fran sat on her bed and it sank even under her slight weight. She picked up the corded phone on the table next to her and scrolled through the caller I.D. The number with a Northern Virginia area code glared at her.

Oh, Lord. I think this is what You want me to do. Give me strength and the right words.

Clicking call, she held her breath.

"Hello?" Faint music played in the background.

Her throat constricted, and her heart jumped at his voice. She swallowed and rolled her shoulders back, mustering courage.

"Hello? Is anyone there?"

"Hello, Stuart."

The music faded. "Fran. Have they found Julie? Is she OK?"

"I–" She cleared her throat. "I thought you'd want to know they have a strong lead. Officer Cooper is going in to get her tonight."

"Just Officer Cooper? By himself? That's good, right?"

"I don't know." Neither Marta nor Luke had given any details. Why hadn't she asked? Surely, he wouldn't go in alone.

"Well, either way, it's good. Julie's OK. They'll bring her home."

"I'm hanging onto that."

Stuart didn't respond and silence filled the line and the room. She didn't have anything else to say to him. She wrapped the phone cord around her fingers.

"Will you call me when you see Julie? Let me know she's OK?"

"There's a good chance it'll be late." She glanced at the clock. Only twenty minutes had passed since Marta's call. Time was creeping.

"No matter what time, it'll be OK."

"OK."

"Thanks, Fran."

"Stuart?" She rushed on, afraid she'd lose her nerve. "When this is over, Julie may not want to see you, but I would like to contact Rebecca."

"I don't expect anything from Julie. I just want to know she's OK." He was silent a moment. "I'll do my best to get you in touch with Rebecca. I want you to be forewarned, though. She's very angry."

"I'll take angry. I've worked through that before. I've waited too long. I owe it to Rebecca to be her mom after messing it up so badly."

"I understand."

Fran guessed he did. She said her good-byes and pushed herself off the bed. For the first time in a long time, she dug out the yellowing envelope from the bottom of her pajama drawer. Breaking the seal, she slid her finger along the flap and gingerly pulled the two pictures out. They were the only two she took from the house when she left Stuart. One showed a proud big sister Rebecca holding Julia when she was about three months old. She stroked the likeness of her oldest daughter's cheek. Happiness still reigned in the girl's hazel eyes. The second picture showed anger and sadness reflected from those same eyes. This time older, framed by a pageboy haircut of a fourteen-year-old Rebecca.

She should have seen it. Recognized the pain her daughter was in and rescued her, too. She should have left the first time Stuart hit her. Should have. The two words the counselors at the women's shelter told her not to dwell on. She'd made the right choice by getting out. Mulling over every time she didn't leave would destroy her healing process.

She slid the pictures back in the envelope and tucked it back into its home. Marta's laughter reached into her room and reminded Fran she had guests to prepare for.

Finding Marta and Luke in the kitchen laughing shed a few pounds of grief off her shoulders.

"Well, look who joined us." Marta stood and embraced her with her large arms. "I was entertaining Luke with the story of Terrence's first experience with the law. He wasn't on the side he's on now."

Fran took a step back, surprise filling her. "Really?"

Marta chuckled. "He was seven and helped himself to a candy bar at the checkout at the grocery store. Fortunately, a neighbor who also was a cop saw the whole thing. He scared Terrence to death then took him under his wing."

She grinned. "I can see that having an impact."

She squeezed her friend's hand. "Thanks for coming, Marta."

"Of course. That's what friends are for. I hear we're having an old-fashioned prayer party tonight, just like the disciples when Peter was imprisoned."

"Hadn't thought of that, but yes, we have more friends coming over."

"Good thing I brought my famous chicken and rice casserole. And these beans here."

She hadn't noticed the pan of green beans Marta stirred on the table until she mentioned them. "Company and food. I'm sorry it took this to get to know you, Marta."

"Me, too. But God always has good plans despite evil." She grabbed the bowl and ambled to the stove. "Pans in here?" she asked, opening the drawer below the oven. "Yep. This one ought to do."

Marveling at Marta's instant comfort in her kitchen, Fran's mind leapt ahead to dessert. She opened the cupboard, examining its contents. Brownies. That would satisfy both the adults and the kids and wouldn't be too much work. Relief at not having to come up with dinner for everyone wafted through her as she pulled the box down and turned to the counter.

Marta hummed as she worked.

Thank You for this friend, Lord. I really needed her right now. But I guess You knew that. She pulled the carton of eggs out of the fridge and went back to the pantry for the oil. "Marta. Can you reach the cabinet to the left of the microwave and hand me a mixing bowl?"

"Sure." Marta gave her an eight-cup glass bowl. "How about some salt and pepper? And some bacon for these beans?"

"Salt and pepper are above the microwave." She opened the refrigerator again, digging into the meat drawer and pulling out a new packet of bacon. "You may want to check the date on that."

Marta checked then proceeded to pull apart the corner flaps.

Cracking three eggs and measuring two tablespoons of oil, Fran glanced over at Luke, sitting at the table. Worry creased his forehead. She stirred in the chocolate powder and looked around the kitchen for a task to give him. The amusement of Marta's story gone, he once again became a lost puppy.

The chime of the doorbell interrupted her thoughts and gave Luke something to do. He popped up out of the chair and strode around the corner. Mark and Sue's voices filtered in from the front foyer.

"Howdy, Hunter. Been fishing lately?" Luke greeted the two-year-old with the same greeting he always did.

"No. Too cold to fish."

"Then hunting."

"No. Too cold to hunt. Me pway twains."

Sue walked in carrying a basket. "Hi, Fran, I brought some munchies."

She couldn't fight the smile. Why had she worried about feeding everyone? "Thanks, Sue." She followed Sue's gaze to Marta, who turned from stirring the green beans. "This is Marta, Officer Cooper's mother. She brought a casserole and beans."

The two ladies shook hands. Sue lifted up her full hands. "Well, I guess we don't need all this. I threw together a veggie tray and brought nuggets for the kids. Heather's bringing meatballs."

"Well, I don't think we'll starve," Marta's booming voice said with humor. "There will be plenty even for a late night snack if it takes that long to hear from Terrence."

Marta's words brought the harsh reality of their gathering back to the forefront.

Fran stopped mid-stir.

Sue's eyes welled with tears.

Hunter's toddler voice drifted from the foyer, explaining to Luke the difference between each train he brought along to play with.

Marta embraced Fran with one arm. "We will eat. We will talk. We will pray. We may even laugh. We won't ignore the seriousness of Julie's situation, but we won't let doubt and discouragement defeat us either."

Fran nodded.

"Now, where can I find a baking dish for those brownies before you stir the chocolate right out of them."

She pointed to the right cabinet, and Marta pulled a nine by thirteen dish out. Sue uncovered the vegetable tray and poured ranch dressing into a bowl she'd brought. The doorbell chimed, the voices of their other friends filled the room, and Fran let the activity push her along through the moments.

TWENTY-THREE

Julie's body ached as nausea pulled her from a fitful sleep. Taking deep breaths to warrant off the waves of sickness brought sharp pains in her left side where she'd been punched. At least he hadn't tied her back down. Shoving herself off the bed and ignoring the throbbing bruises on both her thighs, she lunged to the bathroom, hanging her head over the toilet barely in time. Pain shot through her torso as her stomach emptied its contents.

Leaning back, she wiped her mouth with toilet paper and flushed while trying to steady her breathing. Tears rolled down her cheeks, but she held back the sobs that would cause more pain. Slowly, she reached and pulled herself up to the sink. Handfuls of water rinsed out her mouth and refreshed her.

Oh, Lord. Help me.

She dragged herself back to the small bed with the too-soft mattress and collapsed. What was he doing now? How mad was he? How was she going to get out of this mess? Questions swirled and weariness took over her aching muscles. She had almost drifted back to sleep when the nausea hit again. Deep breaths staved it off but brought the pain back. Finally, she gave up and dashed to the bathroom again.

She hadn't thought anything could have been left, but she heaved several times before the involuntary stomach contractions became dry heaves. This time after wiping her mouth and flushing, she collapsed on the floor. The cold of the linoleum felt good on her cheek and forehead. She closed her eyes.

Feeling Todd's presence brought her around again. He glared at her from the bathroom doorway. "What's going on? What's wrong with you?"

"I...I don't know. I'm sick."

"Don't lie to me. How could you be sick this long? You were fine three days ago."

She had been fine. Living her life without him.

Todd jerked her up by the arm and dragged her back into the bedroom. Flinging her onto the bed, he fumed. "You're lying to me. You're not sick. I bet you didn't even need to go to the store the other day. What I can't figure out is why. Just to keep me away?"

Julie bit her tongue but held her gaze steady. She would not let it show. She would not be afraid.

The red in Todd's face deepened, and he backhanded her. "What are you hiding?"

Stars flashed across her vision. Salty flavor in her mouth suggested blood. When her eyes refocused, he lifted her work costume from the corner where he'd tossed it and shook it. "Where is it? What are you hiding?"

He stomped into the bathroom. The shower curtain scraped back and something crashed, most likely the tension-held rod. He growled then returned to the bedroom. He ran his hands around the edges of the mattress between it and the box spring. Julie curled her legs onto the bed out of his way. Her heart sped up as he reached for the dresser. Yanking open the top drawer, he stopped.

He lifted the plastic bag and looked inside it. The truth of what he found registered in his face. His eyes narrowed to slits as he turned toward her. He held the offending positive pregnancy test between his fingers.

"This is what you're hiding? You're pregnant with his baby? How dare you!" He flung the pregnancy test across the room and lunged.

Julie jerked her knees up and wrapped her arms around them, protecting her stomach from his assault.

"You're mine, not his. You got that. I'll take care of that baby, you lying–"

Holding on as tight as she could, she blocked out his words. He hit her face and back and arms, but nothing caused her to flinch or protect any other part of her body. The most precious part God had planted securely, and she wasn't leaving any chance that Todd was going to take anything else away from her.

When he shoved her and she rolled to the floor without loosening her grip the slightest, he kicked her already injured side and stormed out. She gave into the sobs and did her best to ignore the shooting pain, now not only pulsing through her side and back, but also ringing in her ears.

Thank You. Oh, thank You, Lord. Help me to continue to protect my baby.

She flinched when the outside door slammed. The tears slowed, and she gingerly unfolded her body. Pain seared through her. She couldn't tell where it began or where it ended. She pulled herself up and plopped down on the edge of the bed. She tried to think, failing at her attempt to ignore the throbbing that now included her whole head.

The bedroom door was open. He'd gone out the front door. What was he doing? Maybe she could get out.

Her first attempt to stand told her trying to run would be futile. Besides not having a clue where she was, her body had been through too much in the last twenty-four hours, both from the inside and out. She had no strength to continue sitting, much less stand and run.

"God, I trust You in this. You have an answer I can't see. I know You're with me. Help me hang on until Your answer comes through."

She scooted back on the bed and laid on her left side, cradling her stomach protectively.

~*~

"There's movement."

Clark's crackly message came over the radio and Terrence stopped the car behind Simpson's.

Simpson spoke next. "What kind of movement?"

"The guy matching Todd's picture went in the bedroom a couple minutes ago. All we could see is his pacing back and forth, crossing the window a few times. He's ticked about something, ranting. Then we heard a door. Assuming it's the one in the front and not the one in the house, he's outside."

Terrence depressed the button on his radio. "Did we find out anything else? Have you seen Julie?"

"No, but most of his tirade seemed to focus on the spot in the bedroom between the two windows. I'll wager there's a bed or something where he's holding her."

Taking in the new information, he ran it through the database of every scenario he'd been through in his mind. None of them had Adams outside when they arrived.

"Mattern, what do you think?"

"I don't think it'll change much. He'll hear us coming and retreat back inside. His already being upset might actually be to our advantage. He won't be able to plan clearly if his feathers are already ruffled."

Terrence tapped the steering wheel and looked over at Patterson who shrugged his shoulders. He talked into the radio again. "Mattern says go ahead. We'll go slowly and be prepared for anything. Even for the guy to fire on us as we approach."

"Got it."

The brake lights on Simpson's car went dark and he inched forward. Terrence followed.

"Watts is staying in place," Clark reported. "I'm moving to the west, Heath east. We'll let you know if anything changes."

The radio went silent as the gravel crunched under the car tires. They weren't exactly going into this confrontation blind, but Adams certainly had the advantage. One Terrence didn't like or trust.

He thought for sure they'd traveled the half a mile the property layout showed the driveway's length to be. They crept along the wood-lined lane, weaving around potholes and around sharp turns. The cabin came into view as they crested a hill.

Adams' head shot up at the sound of the approaching cars. He scowled, spun around, and dashed back into the house before Simpson or Terrence pulled to a stop. They parked the cruisers about a hundred yards from the cabin at an angle, putting the nose of each car pointing toward the other's.

The radio crackled. "Was that Adams heading back in?"

"Yes. I'd say we spooked him," Simpson answered.

"He hasn't turned back up where I can see him yet," Watts reported.

Simpson and Mattern met Terrence, Amory, and Patterson in the space between the cars.

"At least he didn't shoot at us." Terrence's hand rested on his weapon.

Mattern rubbed a hand over his hairless head. "Yeah. Now to get him to talk to us."

Stroking his goatee, Simpson eyed the house. "Everything's quiet."

Cold seeped into Terrence's coat, and he rubbed

his gloved hands together. He reached into the now open car window and grabbed the radio. "Watts, you see anything yet?"

"Nothing here. Heath? Clark?"

The next static-hindered voice belonged to Heath. "I've got nothin'."

Clark broke in. "I can see him moving around in the front room, but that's about all I can tell."

Terrence clapped Mattern on the back. "All right. You're on. Show us some magic."

~*~

The door slammed closed. Julie shuddered and braced herself for more of Todd's wrath. The smack didn't come. Peeking over her shoulder at the open door, he paced in the front room. He certainly hadn't cooled off any. He stopped and glared at her. An involuntary shiver coursed through her as she hugged her legs closer to her chest.

"Who did you tell?"

She looked up with wide eyes. "Tell what?"

He stomped toward her. "That I had you. How'd you tell someone at the store? You couldn't have called anyone before I tossed your phone out the window. How'd you do it?"

"I didn't say anything. You watched me the whole time."

"You're lying just like you lied about being sick

and what you needed at the store." His face once again became dark red, contrasting the white of his knuckles as he balled his fists.

"I didn't. I had no chance."

He looked behind him then turned back to Julie. "Then how did they know you were here?"

"They?" Confusion and hope mixed with pain as she pushed herself to a sitting position. The pain took her breath.

"Them. The cops that pulled up the drive. How else would they know?"

She kept her breaths shallow and knees close. "You took me, Todd. Ripped me right out of my life. I have a mother, a husband, and friends. Did you really think they wouldn't notice I'd gone missing?"

"But you're mine." He pounded the doorframe, accenting his words.

"I'm not yours, Todd. I haven't been for a long time. My friends and family love me, and I'm sure they reported me missing. Don't you think the police follow up on things like that?" She spoke slowly and feasted on her own words. She'd determined to trust God, to believe that someone was out there looking for her. Now she had proof. She hadn't been abandoned. Their love filled her with courage.

"But I have no connection to this cottage. How did they find me if you didn't say anything?"

For someone intelligent in many ways, that had to be the stupidest question she'd ever heard him ask. "Police investigate. They find information. That's what they do. Isn't there someone who knew where you were going?"

Todd's eyes narrowed. "Bubba. I'll kill him."

"You have to get out of here first."

"You'd like me to just give up, wouldn't you?"

"Todd Adams," a booming voice sounding like it came through a megaphone interrupted her answer. "This is Burt Watts with the state police. We'd like to talk to you."

He stood perfectly still, his eyes trained on her.

The voice from outside blared again. "We need to know that Julie Montgomery's OK."

Panic flickered on his face. He steeled it again. "This is your fault."

"You took me."

He pulled the gun from the back of his waist and aimed it at her. "You left me. You started this."

"Todd." The persistent intrusion filtered in again. "We're going to leave a radio by the front door."

TWENTY-FOUR

Food eaten, leftovers stored away, dishes cleaned, and five children ranging from age two to seven tucked away watching a movie in the spare bedroom, the adults gathered in Fran's living room. She dropped into her favorite chair. At Marta's suggestion, they had gathered the seats and chairs into a circle. She grabbed Marta's hand in her left and Dawn's in her right.

"Now, we pray."

Six heads bowed, before she bowed her own. In the silence, her heart cried out, groaning unspoken prayers her mouth refused to utter.

Marta's deep voice came low and steady. "Lord, You are holy. Magnificent. Omniscient. All-powerful. We come here together to lift up our sister, Julie. You know what is going on with her, Lord. You see her distress in this moment. We are here feeling very helpless, but know that with You on our side, nothing is impossible. Watch over Terrence and the other officers dedicated to bringing Julie home. Give them wisdom and bring her peace in these last moments of her captivity. We implore You to bring her home and heal all involved in this situation."

Amens filled the room. Then silence.

"Father," Mark took over after a few moments. "You call us Your children and show us love in everything You do. Surround us now with Your love in these uncertain moments. We praise You and thank You that You are here with us even in this."

Fran's chest ached. Pressure bore down making it difficult for her to breathe. She silently raised up every word of prayer uttered for Julie. She believed every one of them. Yet, the oppression weighing on her felt heavier by the minute.

Oh, God. What is it? Has something changed?

She pulled her hand from Marta's and covered her face. The room grew silent and thick. She slid her hands down to her heart, as if pressure from the outside would relieve the heaviness from within. Questioning eyes and furrowed eyebrows met her gaze.

Marta set her hand on her knee. "What is it?"

"Something's wrong."

Luke leaned forward. "What do you mean?"

She took a deep breath in and blew it out. "They're going in. But there's something else. Julie's in danger." She tapped her breastbone. "I can feel it."

No one answered her fears. Marta closed her eyes, her mouth moving in inaudible prayers.

Mark stood and strode over to the front window, staring out of it, jaw twitching.

A single tear burned its way down Fran's cheek,

and she held her breath.

Mark turned. "I feel it, too. But–"

She exhaled. "But?"

"They're going in. They've backed this guy into a corner. Combatants don't back down or flee in response to danger. They raise their backs and fight," Mark answered.

Luke's face crumbled. "So, you're saying Julie's in more danger now because the police are there to rescue her?"

Fran watched Luke closely as Mark answered.

"Yes."

Her hands shook. "We've finally gotten good news. They've found Julie. But instead of being relieved we need to worry more?"

Marta spoke up. "No, Fran, we don't worry more. We keep praying."

"That's right." Sue pushed herself out of her chair, protruding belly first, stood by Mark, and grabbed his hand. "God's bigger than this, remember?"

Marta's arm wrapped around Fran, holding her up. "God's telling you something. His Spirit is here, letting you know this battle's more than between the police and this lunatic. We do not wage war against men but against principalities and darkness."

Hope filtered through Fran's tight chest. "Yes. We can't be with Julie now, but God can." She met Marta's deep-set, coffee-colored eyes. "Keep reminding me. I just want my Julie home."

"I know." Marta waved the group closer and each one gathered around Fran.

Luke knelt beside her, his eyes red with anguish. More than a dozen hands laid on her back, shoulders, and knees, as well as Luke's. She basked in the continued prayers lifted up by the shaky, yet confident voice of her new friend.

~*~

Todd kept the gun trained on Julie. Her heart raced and her entire body shook, but she refused to show him the terror coursing through her veins. "They left a radio, Todd. They want to talk with you."

His face contorted in a snarl, the right side of his lips raising more than the left. "They don't want to talk. They want me to let you go."

"Give them a chance. They can help you get what you want."

"I want you," he yelled. He raised the gun, pointing it at her head. "If they aren't willing to leave us alone, neither of us will walk out of here."

She fought the involuntary shudder and squeezed her eyes shut for a second to regain control. "You're not thinking straight, Todd. What do you mean to happen? We live out here in the woods for the next fifty years? I don't work; you don't work? That's not a life."

He strode forward. "No. We go somewhere else. Start over. Leave everything else behind. As long as we're together, it doesn't matter where."

"But I don't love you, Todd. Doesn't that mean anything?"

His hands shot up to his head, the side of the gun pressed against his temple. "Don't say that. It's not true. They've brainwashed you."

The muffled crackle of a two-way radio came from outside the cabin. The words were indistinguishable. How long would they give him? Could they even tell what was going on? The two tiny windows on either side of the bed couldn't afford much of a view from outside. He seemed to be avoiding the front room, where the only decent-sized window allowed visual access. She had to keep him talking.

She lowered her voice. "No. You tried to brainwash me."

He pointed the gun back at her. "What did you say?"

"I said you tried to brainwash me. Just like your dad tried to brainwash you."

His face reddened. "You don't know what you're talking about."

"I may not have been the smartest girl in class, Todd, but I recognize signs of abuse."

"Shut up."

"We were together for years. We were...we were close. Do you think I missed the burn marks? Cigarettes leave distinctive scars."

His left hand shot up and rubbed the outside of his right bicep.

"I saw the strap marks on the back of your legs, too."

He dropped his left arm and steadied the gun. "Stop. That has nothing to do with this."

"Love doesn't have to hurt. Love is not supposed to hurt."

He looked around, his eyes clouding over. He studied the outer room, took one step in that direction, and stopped. "That's enough. I'm not going to talk to them, and I won't talk to you anymore."

"My dad hit me, too."

Todd's eyes flashed.

"That's not love. Love gives; it doesn't take. Or control. Or push."

"I told you to shut up. I love you. I've spent every day since you left thinking of you, wanting you, missing you. That's love."

"Thinking of me, Todd? Or planning, conniving, and figuring out a way to get back your control?"

He crossed the room in three steps and struck her across the face with the gun.

~*~

Terrence eyed the radio still sitting outside the door of the cabin. "He's not coming to get it."

Mattern rubbed a hand over his slick head and nodded agreement. "He's refusing to talk. Hard to negotiate one-sided."

"He doesn't want to negotiate. There's nothing we have to offer him. I'd wager everything he wants is already inside." He picked up his radio. "Clark."

"Copy."

"You still have eyes?"

"Yes. He's angry, threatening. He pulled a gun on

her, but they're talking."

Simpson leaned over. "Now do you think we should go in? This crazy has a gun."

Terrence raised his chin. "We go in too soon, Julie gets hurt."

"We go in too late, Julie ends up dead," Simpson replied.

Meeting the older man's glare, Terrence didn't waver. Everything came down to the right timing. He'd spent too much effort and energy finding Julie Montgomery to let this pompous control hog put her in danger.

The radio crackled. "There's movement."

He waited for Clark to continue.

"He's out of sight."

The crackling silenced and Terrence fought the urge to bust the door down. A bird chirped, signaling the rest of the world continued moving on as the group of officers waited. A twig snapped as Amory shifted his wait. Terrence shot him a look then returned his glare to the door. What was going on? Adams knew the police were there. He'd refused to talk to them. Maybe Julie was smart enough to buy them time. Of course, she wouldn't know exactly where they were or what they planned to do.

If only they had a way to communicate with her. Get him back in our view, Julie.

"He's moved back by the door," Clark's voice broke the silence.

Terrence sighed with relief. No gunshot. They still had time. But what had occurred in those quiet moments? "Simpson."

"What?"

"We need an ambulance here, waiting," Terrence advised.

Simpson stroked his graying goatee. "You ready to move?"

"Just about. He's escalating. What are the chances Mrs. Montgomery has escaped injury so far? He may not be ready to shoot yet, but his violent streak is definitely showing."

"He moves in, smacks her around a little to feel in control?"

"That's what I'm thinking," Terrence agreed.

Simpson pulled out his cell. "I'll call it in."

Terrence stopped him. "Give them the address, but tell the driver to stay at the end of the driveway. We don't need any more bodies in firing range. And no sirens. No lights."

Simpson dialed. "This is Chief Simpson. We need two ambulances at 72625 Bird's Eye Lane. Have them come in quiet, no sirens, no lights. Instruct the drivers to pull into the gravel driveway off the main road, but not to advance until you hear from us again." He listened, nodded, and hung up.

Terrence raised a brow. "Two?"

"He's after Mrs. Montgomery. We're after him. I like being prepared."

Terrence cocked his head in acknowledgement. He considered the possibility that thirty years on the force didn't get you just an obnoxious attitude. "How long will it take them to get here?"

"About ten minutes," Simpson replied.

"OK. We keep an eye on Adams and don't act until we have to." He depressed the radio button. "Clark. Got an update?"

"He's holding up the doorframe," Clark's voice came through.

Terrence drummed his fingers on his leg. "No movement?"

"Not in the last few minutes."

"How are Watts and Heath holding up?"

The line went silent. He imagined Clark was signaling the other two officers. The radio crackled again. "Holding up all right."

"As long as he doesn't move, we wait," Terrence instructed. "We've called in ambulances to be prepared before we move. Tell Watts to stay alert and radio if anything changes."

"Copy."

~*~

Julie's hand covered the swelling bruise on her right cheek. Tears stung her eyes and fell when she squeezed them shut. The pain reverberated through her pounding head. But it also reminded her she was still alive, and he hadn't come after her baby.

She shifted her weight and winced. Reality gripped her heart tighter than the ropes had her wrists days before. He hadn't pulled the trigger. Yet.

He stood leaning against the doorjamb. She didn't recognize the look on his face. His forehead was furled, and his lips pulled tight. His eyes darted from room to room, window to window. Was that fear? She knew that emotion. She should recognize it in another.

He gripped the gun, but his arm hung down by his side. The fingers on his other hand drummed against his thigh.

If he was scared, she could use that. Surely, he wasn't ready to die. Had he even considered the possibility of how all this might end? At least she had God. In all this, she wasn't alone. Hadn't God reminded her of His presence over and over throughout the last few days?

She closed her eyes, shutting out the harshness of reality. *Lord, thank You for keeping me in Your arms through all this. I know the police are here and You've provided a way out for me. Please hold me tighter now and make it clear what I'm to do and say. Protect everyone involved and help to soften Todd's heart.*

She opened her eyes. Todd hadn't moved. His eyes continued to shift from side to side, but he avoided looking at her. Wincing and biting her lip against the pain, she sat up.

"Todd." She kept her voice steady and low.

"What?"

"Things don't have to be this way."

He turned his head and glared at her. "Are you ready to tell them you're here willingly? Then it doesn't have to be like this."

Shock ripped through her. Was he really that delusional? "No."

In response, he shoved off the doorframe and

raised the gun at her again. "You belong to me," he spat.

"I don't belong to you or anyone else."

His eyebrows shot up. "So, your man doesn't even know how to treat you so you know you're his, huh?"

"My husband loves and respects me, but he doesn't own me. The only One I belong to is God."

Todd snorted. "God. There is no God."

"There is. I didn't know Him when we were together, but I do now."

His face reddened.

She swallowed the lump of fear in her throat. "That's how I found out what real love is. This isn't love."

"I love you! Why can't you see that?"

Julie laced her fingers and squeezed her hands together. "Could be the gun you keep pointing at me."

"Real love doesn't give up," he yelled. "If you really loved me, you wouldn't have left. I never stopped loving you."

"You never loved me. You just wanted to control me."

"Shut up. Shut up. Shut up."

TWENTY-FIVE

Terrence glanced at Simpson. "You hear that?"

Simpson's finger played with his holster button. "Yeah. Sounds like he's escalating."

Terrence grabbed the radio. "Clark. What do you have for eyes?"

Seconds ticked. He pictured the three officers around the back of the cabin talking to each other in signalese.

"Watts is in place. He's got a clear view of the subject."

He knew what that meant. If they were ready to go in, Watts could take Adams out if needed. "How's Adams look? Think he's about done?"

The radio crackled. "He's not backing down. That's for sure. Has he communicated at all?"

"No."

The definite word reverberated around him. He met Simpson's hard stare.

Simpson unholstered his gun and signaled Amory, Patterson, and Mattern to do the same. Terrence nodded and pulled out his weapon.

"Clark. We're ready. You still have eyes?"

"Affirmative."

"Tell Watts to get ready. You and Heath meet us around front."

"Done."

"Silence radios." He threw his on the driver's seat. Clark wouldn't answer. He'd already be moving toward them. Adrenaline replaced the blood in Terrence's veins. His knuckles gripped his piece. He couldn't control what he'd meet on the other side of the cabin door, but he could control himself.

Pointing to each officer and giving them a number of order to move in, as well as a location once they reached the outside of the cabin, Terrence crept forward. He didn't so much as glance behind him, but knew Simpson, Patterson, and Amory followed him. Mattern took up the rear and headed toward the side of the one window housed in the front of the aged building. He caught Heath and Clark in his peripheral view.

At the door, he reached up and tested it. He'd had no doubt it'd be locked but preferred not to use his body to bust through. He pointed at Mattern, held up two fingers to his eyes, and aimed them back at Mattern.

The bald head nodded. He held up one finger, then five.

Fifteen feet.

Mattern's eyes shifted back and forth quickly.

He was watching for them.

Raising his arm, the negotiator let them know Julie Montgomery sat at the most vulnerable position possible.

Terrence nodded and stood. He called Amory, the bulkiest officer present, forward with a hand wave. He inhaled calm, holding himself back from acting too quickly. The urge to wrap this case up surged through his muscles.

The time had come.

He caught each man's eye then focused on Amory. He pointed at the ex-football player, himself, and the door. He held up five fingers. Assuring nods answered his silent command as each officer took his attack stance.

One finger closed, then a second, third, fourth, and the last. With a swift movement, the bulk of Terrence and Amory collided with the hundred-year-old door. The door was strong and pain ripped through Terrence's shoulder as the doorframe gave way with a loud crack.

"Police. Drop your weapon," Terrence demanded.

Adams snarled at him, spun to face the inner room, and pulled his trigger.

Julie screamed, and Terrence, his gun trained on Adams' torso, shot an instant later, echoed by a sniper bullet piercing the window in the unseen room.

TWENTY-SIX

Terrence leapt over Todd Adams' slumped body and raced to the bed Julie lay in. Blood seeped through the left side of her shirt. "No." He didn't come through all this, work so hard to lose her now. Holstering his gun, he yanked up the sheet, balled it up and pressed it against her shoulder. She groaned and squirmed.

Behind him, Patterson spoke into his radio. "Two citizens down. Get those medics in here immediately."

Glancing back, he spotted his partner lean over the perpetrator and test his pulse at the neck. Patterson answered the unasked question. "He's alive, but barely. How is she?"

Terrence repeated the gesture on Julie. Her pulse was strong. Her eyes fluttered. "Hi, Mrs. Montgomery. I'm Officer Cooper. You're going to be OK. Your husband and mom know we're here to get you. They're waiting for me to call."

She mumbled something and he leaned closer, noticing the bruises on her face for the first time.

"Luke. Baby."

Tears welled in his eyes. "Yes, Luke. He misses you terribly and is ready for you to come home."

"What do we have here?" An EMT stepped up to the bed.

Terrence moved up by the headboard, keeping the pressure on Julie's shoulder while allowing the medic space to move in. "Gunshot wound, seems to be her left shoulder. Some bruising on her face. Haven't had a chance to investigate further injuries."

A second medic moved in on her right side and nodded toward the doorway. "There's no way we're going to get the gurney in here. Even once he's moved. We're going to have to carry her."

Terrence, relieved from his holding pressure duty, pulled the fitted sheet out from between the mattress and box springs. "Between the four of us, we should be able to support her and squeeze through. Let's go."

The first medic pointed at Patterson. "You get the bottom right. Hold the sheet as close to her body as you can. We need to keep her as stationary as possible. You–"

"I know, I take bottom left."

"Yes, but stagger yourself. That way only one of us goes through the door at a time."

Two interminable minutes later, at Terrence's best guess, they placed Julie on the gurney to be lifted into the ambulance. The back doors slammed shut. He sprinted to the driver side door. "What hospital?"

"MCV."

He nodded, and the ambulance took off down the gravel lane. A hand clamped on his shoulder.

Patterson met his gaze. "You go. We'll wrap things up here. The paperwork will wait for you." He grinned. "All piled up in a successful case sort of way on your desk when you get in tomorrow."

"You sure?"

"Of course. You have the contact information for the husband and mom. Go. Give them the good news, and see how she's doing. Besides, that'll need to be a part of the report, too."

"OK. I'll touch base later." In his car, Terrence waited until he turned on the paved road to pull out his cellphone. His hand shook.

God, you have no reason to listen to me, but please let Julie Montgomery live.

He breathed in calm and exhaled the remnants of adrenaline. They'd found her. Alive. The purples and blues of her face flashed in his mind. They'd arrived just in time.

Stopped at a light, Terrence dialed his mom's number before turning on the main road toward Richmond.

"Terrence?"

"We got her, Mom." Tears choked his words. He swallowed hard before continuing, "We found her. She's injured, but OK." Hopefully, she was OK.

"Woo-hoo. Hallelujah. Praise the Lord. They found her. They found her."

Terrence laughed at the shouting, and the praises to God he heard in the background. He guessed his mom was with Fran and Luke.

Her voice came back on the line. "I'm so glad,

honey. Where should Fran and Luke meet her, or are you bringing her home?"

His grin faded. "No. She's been shot, Mom. In the shoulder; It's probably not too serious, but they had to take her to the hospital." They'd have taken her to the hospital anyway for a full examination, especially given the bruises.

"Oh, Terrence. But she's OK. You're sure."

"I..." He couldn't lie to his mom. "I'm pretty sure. Tell them to get on the road, though. Head to MCV and keep praying."

"I will."

He hung up. At least he didn't have to tell Fran or Luke personally. He'd gotten emotional enough on the phone with his own mother. What was happening to him? He'd be glad when this day ended and he could go back to his detached detective's life.

~*~

"I'd like to see Julie Montgomery, please."

"Are you family?"

Terrence leaned on the counter. "No. I'm the police officer who just rescued her. I need to know how she's doing. For my report."

The nurse with a tight bun in her hair and dark blue uniform clicked away on the keyboard with her short, but perfectly manicured fingernails. Her gaze scanned the screen then met his. "She's been taken to X-ray. Sorry, you'll have to wait."

"Is there anyone I can talk to?"

"Sorry, no. I'll alert her nurse that someone's here."

He pulled his lips into a thin line and turned from the desk. Two steps later, he spun. "Oh, how about Todd Adams? He's part of the case, too."

Her fingers once again flew on the keys. She blinked twice then looked up. "You'll have to see a doctor about him. I'll let them know."

He paced the waiting room. Couples sat huddled, mothers caressed red-eyed children, and in one corner a family of five whispered. Thirty more minutes would pass before Fran and Luke arrived. Well, if they obeyed the speed limit. In this instance, he wouldn't blame them for pushing the boundaries to get there.

"Excuse me, Officer?"

Turning, Terrence faced a young doctor. "Yes. Officer Cooper."

"I'm Dr. Wilde. You asked about Todd Adams?"

He nodded. "I did. He's involved in a case I'm working."

"Can we go over here to talk?" The man nudged his head toward an empty corner by the door leading to the E.R.

"Sure."

Once in the more secluded, private space, the doctor adjusted his glasses, pushing them back up his thin nose. "Mr. Adams died en route."

Terrence's shoulders relaxed. "We knew it didn't look good."

"So you were on the scene?"

"Yes, sir. And we're going to need a full report.

Can I get some contact information to pass on to my chief?"

"Of course." He cleared his throat. "There was also a young lady."

"Yes." Terrence leaned in. "Mrs. Montgomery. How is she?"

"She'll pull through. The wounds are mostly superficial. A couple of broken ribs, we think. The bullet didn't pierce anything critical. She's lost quite a bit of blood, of course, but not a life-threatening amount. At least not for her."

Cocking his head to the side, Terrence furrowed his brows. "Not to her?"

"Yes. Whenever a mother experiences trauma such as Mrs. Montgomery has, it puts her in high risk of miscarrying."

"Miscarry?"

"You didn't know? Well, it's not too surprising. She's only about six weeks along. I'm just grateful she woke enough to warn us before we took her to X-ray."

"Yeah." Terrence shook his head. The surprises kept coming. "Um, her family should be here soon. Will they be able to see her?"

"Most likely. We're going to admit her. She won't get a room for a few hours. Then she'll stay a couple days so we can monitor the baby. Let the receptionist know when they arrive."

"Thanks, Dr. Wilde. I will."

Terrence leaned against the wall. Pregnant, kidnapped, beaten, and shot. He'd be amazed if Julie Montgomery came through this in one piece mentally.

But she had survived. And that's what he'd prayed for.

TWENTY-SEVEN

Luke rushed through the automatic doors to the reception desk. Resisting the urge to cut in line, he waited behind the Latina woman with a crying baby on her hip. Come on. He needed to see his wife. He silently pleaded with them to hurry.

A hand rested on his arm and he spun to face Officer Cooper. "Luke, she's OK. She's waiting for you. Follow the ER signs and just ask a nurse which room she's in."

"Thanks." He turned his gaze back at Fran, followed by Marta, Mark, Sue, Paul, Dawn, Craig, and Heather.

"Go," his mother-in-law insisted through shimmering tears. "We'll be here. You go see your wife first."

Nodding, he turned and strode across the polished floor. He pushed through the door under the Emergency Room sign. People in uniforms milled everywhere. A few people stood in doorways and a couple of orderlies pushed a gurney down the hallway.

Julie. He had to find Julie.

"Excuse me, sir. Can I help you?" The pretty blonde nurse stopped in front of him.

"My wife." He gulped. "Julie Montgomery. Where is she?"

She smiled, showing off matching dimples and shiny white teeth. "Of course. She's been asking for you. This way."

He saw nothing else until he arrived at a door that opened to the most stunning vision he'd ever seen. He rushed across the room, covering his wife's smile with kisses. Pulling back, he noticed dark spots on her face and the bandage covering her shoulder which poked out of a sling on her left arm. "Oh, Julie. What in the world happened?"

"It doesn't matter. I'm here. You're here. We're alive."

He grasped her right hand, gazing into her beautiful face. He'd almost lost her. She was back and safe, but something still stood between them. He leaned in and brushed her lips with his then looked her in the eye. "Why did you keep all this from me? You could have trusted me with it."

Her eyes fluttered. She inhaled deeply. "I know. I didn't trust me. I thought if I ignored it all, acted like it never happened, I could pretend it was a bad dream."

Maybe it truly hadn't been about him. She had so many demons to contend with. He didn't think he'd have chosen to keep everything secret that she did, but suddenly it didn't matter.

"My darling, Julie." He kissed her once more. "I'll

never let you out of my sight again. I couldn't bear it if I lost you for good."

She laughed. "You will let me out of your sight. And we'll be OK."

He stared at his wife. She was laughing. Despite everything that had happened over the last few days. His heart felt like it would burst. "You are marvelous. After everything you've been through, you're even more radiant and beautiful than ever."

She squeezed his hand. "I'm free, Luke. Free from my past. I'll tell you everything. We'll work through every bump and trial together."

His joy overflowed in a long, deep kiss. He pulled away. He didn't want to move. Or let her go, ever. "I should go get your mom now. She's anxious to see you."

"Not yet."

He raised his eyebrows. "No?"

"No. In keeping with my promise to tell you everything, there's something I need to say."

His heart raced. Did her injuries go beyond what he saw? If that monster hurt her in other ways, if he–

"Luke. The news is good."

His tongue stuck to the roof of his mouth. Good news. In the midst of all this. He had a hard time believing it was possible

"We're going to have a baby, Luke. I'm pregnant."

His nose burned and his eyes filled. A baby. "You're pregnant? Now? It's OK?"

Happy tears sprinkled her smile. "Yes. They're going to keep us a few days to make sure, but he or she seems fine so far. A strong heartbeat every time they check."

"A baby." He jumped up and pumped his arm in the air. "Wahoo."

"Shh," Julie said through a bubbling laugh.

The dimpled, blonde nurse poked her head in the door.

Shaking his head, Luke answered her unspoken question. "Everything's OK. Great, actually. We're going to have a baby."

The dimples deepened. "Congratulations."

He turned to his wife. "Can I go get them now?"

She leaned back against the pillow. "Yes."

EPILOGUE

Terrence had never seen anything like it before. Or maybe he hadn't paid attention. His eyes had opened to so much over the last month.

Julie and Luke Montgomery stood across the crowded room surrounded by friends and loved ones celebrating her safe return home. He kept his mouth from dropping open when Stuart and Pauline Parker walked through the church's fellowship hall, trailed by Darlene and Emma.

"Mom, did you know Julie's dad would be here?"

"Of course, honey. He and Julie have been talking on the phone since she got home from the hospital. He came down yesterday, and they met for dinner."

He shook his head.

"Forgiveness, son, is a wonderful healing property."

Julie's gaze traveled to her father and his new family, and she smiled. Terrence expected her to be a basket case, scared of everything after her ordeal. The woman he studied now held an aura of peace and contentment as she rested her right hand on her stomach, her left still supported by a sling.

Luke and Julie stepped up onto a small stage. She accepted a microphone from a slightly older woman. "Thank you all for coming. Your love and support are overwhelming. We are so grateful God has given us this faith family to surround us during these trying days." She paused, visibly swallowing. "God has provided beyond our expectations. We've shared with a few of you, but feel it's time to reveal the last detail now that we're almost to the end of the first trimester."

Someone behind Terrence gasped.

Her smile grew. "Luke and I are thrilled to announce that in the middle of all of the devil's attempts to bring trouble into our lives, God, who is greater, has given greater. We're expecting a baby late this summer."

Cheers and hallelujahs reverberated off the ceiling and walls. Terrence's cheeks began to hurt from smiling.

"Officer Cooper?"

He turned to face Maggie and his heart leapt into a gallop.

"Hi. Do you remember me? From the shop in CW?"

"Yes, I remember. It's good to see you again."

"You, too. Especially under such happy circumstances this time."

He nodded. His parched mouth refused to utter another sound.

"I was wondering, would you like to get a plate of

food with me? I think Luke and Julie'll be occupied for a while."

Looking back at his mom, not wanting her to feel abandoned, he raised a brow. Her grin shone as big as Julie's as she motioned him toward Maggie.

"Sure. That'd be great."

A Devotional Moment

But whoever does not have them is nearsighted and blind, forgetting that they have been cleansed from their past sins. ~ 2 Peter 1:9

When we ask for forgiveness with a contrite heart, God always forgives, and the ultimate consequence of that sin—death—is paid for by Jesus' sacrifice. Sometimes, however, there are earthly consequences to our choices that cannot be avoided, regardless of the fact that the eternal consequence has been covered by His grace. These consequences can feel debilitating, but if we trust Him, He covers us under sheltering wings and offers us His mercy, and gives us the courage and strength to meet repercussions head-on.

In **In an Instant**, a man has discovered a secret about someone he loves. The devastating consequences threaten to shatter his peace of mind, but a more pressing event has captured his attention, and he has to unravel the threads that hold past sins captive. However, his mission is not without its own consequences.

Have you ever felt as if God hadn't forgiven you?

Perhaps the weight of the lingering consequences of sin keep you pinned down. Understand that if you have truly repented and asked for forgiveness, you are forgiven. It is true that if our sin has affected others, it may be necessary for us to make restitution if time and circumstances allow it, but the haunting remembrance of sin revisits us mostly to be a stumbling block to keep us from God. Confronting the effects of our sins may at first bring chaos, but with time and God's love, it can bring any episode to a close, and we'll never have that sin hanging over us again.

LORD, WHEN THE PAST RETURNS TO HAUNT MY PRESENT, LEAD ME TO COMFORT AND RESOLUTION. IN JESUS' NAME I PRAY, AMEN.

Thank you

We appreciate you reading this Prism title. For other
Christian fiction and clean-and-wholesome stories,
please visit our on-line bookstore at
www.prismbookgroup.com.

For questions or more information, contact us at
customer@pelicanbookgroup.com.

Prism is an imprint of
Pelican Book Group
www.PelicanBookGroup.com

Connect with Us
www.facebook.com/Pelicanbookgroup
www.twitter.com/pelicanbookgrp

To receive news and specials, subscribe to our bulletin
http://pelink.us/bulletin

May God's glory shine through
this inspirational work of fiction.

AMDG

You Can Help!

At Pelican Book Group it is our mission to entertain readers with fiction that uplifts the Gospel. It is our privilege to spend time with you awhile as you read our stories.

We believe you can help us to bring Christ into the lives of people across the globe. And you don't have to open your wallet or even leave your house!

Here are 3 simple things you can do to help us bring illuminating fiction™ to people everywhere.

1) If you enjoyed this book, write a positive review. Post it at online retailers and websites where readers gather. And share your review with us at reviews@pelicanbookgroup.com (this does give us permission to reprint your review in whole or in part.)

2) If you enjoyed this book, recommend it to a friend in person, at a book club or on social media.

3) If you have suggestions on how we can improve or expand our selection, let us know. We value your opinion. Use the contact form on our web site or e-mail us at customer@pelicanbookgroup.com

God Can Help!

Are you in need? The Almighty can do great things for you. Holy is His Name! He has mercy in every generation. He can lift up the lowly and accomplish all things. Reach out today.

Do not fear: I am with you; do not be anxious: I am your God. I will strengthen you, I will help you, I will uphold you with my victorious right hand.

~Isaiah 41:10 (NAB)

We pray daily, and we especially pray for everyone connected to Pelican Book Group—that includes you! If you have a specific need, we welcome the opportunity to pray for you. Share your needs or praise reports at http://pelink.us/pray4us

Free Book Offer

We're looking for booklovers like you to partner with us! Join our team of influencers today and periodically receive free eBooks and exclusive offers.

For more information
Visit http://pelicanbookgroup.com/booklovers